Bethan stiffened, pushing away from him

The sense of belonging in his arms was illusion. Bethan could only feel shame at having forgotten, even momentarily, that he belonged to Siriol now. "I'm sorry," she said. "I didn't mean to embarrass you."

His mouth quirked upward, while his arms seemed reluctant to let her go. "Do I look embarrassed?"

"No, but *I* am." She cast around for something to say to explain her mindless response without exposing her true feelings. "I wouldn't want you to think I was still suffering from the childish infatuation I inflicted on you years ago. You'll have to put my show of feminine weakness down to all the shocks I've received."

She watched the smile die out of his eyes. "Bethan, I don't—"

But she didn't want to listen. "You will thank Siriol, won't you, for loaning me your shoulder to cry on?"

STACY ABSALOM and her "scrumptious" husband, Derek, live on the fringe of a small English village overlooking the rolling Leicestershire countryside. She used to write short stories for women's magazines but now devotes her professional energy exclusively to writing romance novels. In her spare time, of which she has little, she enjoys listening to classical music, knitting very complicated patterns and driving fast cars.

Books by Stacy Absalom

HARLEQUIN ROMANCE
2581—KNAVE OF HEARTS
2671—THE PASSION AND THE PAIN
2689—DARK NIGHT DAWNING

These books may be available at your local bookseller.

Don't miss any of our special offers. Write to us at the following address for information on our newest releases.

Harlequin Reader Service
901 Fuhrmann Blvd., P.O. Box 1397, Buffalo, NY 14240
Canadian address: P.O. Box 603,
Fort Erie, Ont. L2A 5X3

STACY ABSALOM

ishbel's party

Harlequin Books

TORONTO • NEW YORK • LONDON
AMSTERDAM • PARIS • SYDNEY • HAMBURG
STOCKHOLM • ATHENS • TOKYO • MILAN

Harlequin Presents first edition January 1987
ISBN 0-373-10943-1

Original hardcover edition published in 1986
by Mills & Boon Limited

CHAPTER ONE

THE face in the mirror still seemed that of a stranger and gave Bethan Steele a mild shock every time she caught a glimpse of herself. Not that the hospital ward was over-endowed with mirrors, but here in the bathroom where she was now allowed to bath unaided, she wiped the misting of steam away and studied her new image.

The tan acquired by years of working in hot climates had faded during the weeks in the London hospital, but apart from her unfamiliar paleness, from the front her body looked much as it always had done. The breaks in her arm and collar-bone had mended without a trace and her figure was slender and boyish; small, high, tip-tilted breasts, flat stomach, not an ounce of spare flesh on the slight curves of her hips. It was only when she twisted round she could see the disfigurement of her back. The burns had healed well and the plastic surgeon had done a splendid job, but as yet, the scars he had assured her would fade in time were still livid.

It was her hair that had effected the greatest transformation in her appearance. Carroty when she was a child, it had matured to a reddish gold, and because for the last six years she had lived and worked where hairdressing facilities were unknown, she had worn it long, coiled at the back of her head for coolness. But her injuries had necessitated the shaving of her head and though the new growth was hiding the scars on her scalp, it was difficult to accustom herself to the sight of the short, coppery halo of curls framing her small, pointed-chinned face, a face that somehow seemed all eyes.

It made her look nearer eighteen than her actual

twenty-eight years, she thought wryly, which might
have been something to be pleased about if she had
cared about her appearance. But she had always had
more important things to worry about than that. Even
now worry lurked in the depths of her huge, greenish
eyes, and though it was trivial compared to the
heartbreaking problems that usually occupied her
energies in her job as a nurse working for an
international relief agency, she couldn't deny the worry
was there.

It was a new experience for Bethan to be concerned
for herself. Ever since she had qualified as a nurse she
had devoted herself to children in need, offering her
services to the relief agency and going wherever they
sent her, to whatever inhospitable part of the world
where the tide of war and famine had tossed up a
flotsam of unwanted and helpless humanity. She had
been in no position to protest about being brought to
England for medical care after she had been caught in
the blast of an exploding shell in a Beirut street, but she
had always assumed that once she had recovered from
her injuries she would be sent back there, or to some
other distressed part of the world where she could be of
some use. But only two days ago Dr Fielding had
disabused her of that assumption.

Dr Fielding was a director of the relief agency and
Bethan had contacted him as soon as she had been told
her discharge from hospital was imminent. She had
expected a note from him giving her a date and time
when she should call to see him, but he had surprised her
by coming to the hospital to see her, borrowing the
Sister's office to talk to her privately.

After exchanging greetings he said sympathetically, 'I
must say you don't look too bad considering what
you've been through, Bethan. It was rotten luck after
coming unscathed through the siege of Beirut to get
caught up in the fighting again.'

A haunted expression flickered across Bethan's face

as the ugly memory she had disciplined herself to blot out was brought forcibly back. 'At least I'm still alive,' she said in a low voice.

Dr Fielding's grey head nodded in agreement. 'You're referring to your companion who wasn't so lucky. I'm sorry, my dear. It was particularly tragic in the circumstances.'

And particularly unfair, Bethan found herself thinking. If one of them had to die, why couldn't it have been herself? An eye for an eye and a tooth for a tooth ... Why had it had to be Betty-Lou who had led a blameless existence and who had everything to live for? But it was no good brooding on the injustice of fate.

She thrust the black thoughts from her and said briskly, 'Do you want me back in Beirut or is it to be somewhere else this time?'

'I *want* you in any of half a dozen places, Bethan.' He leaned back in his chair, his sharp gaze assessing her shrewdly. 'But I know I'm going to have to wait.'

Bethan frowned. 'I'm sorry, I don't understand. The hospital will be discharging me any day now.'

'So I'm told. But my dear girl, you can't seriously believe you can go straight back to the conditions you usually work under—after the injuries you received?'

Pure cowardice at the thought of the uneasy peace in Beirut that could still bring the city under fire and leave it at the mercy of warring factions, brought a tremor to the hands clasped loosely in her lap before she could bring it under control. 'That's nonsense. I'm perfectly fit now, but if it makes you any happier, I'll have a couple of weeks' holiday before I take up a new assignment.'

She saw his sceptical eyes were on her hands which still betrayed a tremor and she clasped them tighter. But then to her amazement he said, 'All right, Bethan, that's all for now. You can go.'

She stared at him blankly. 'Go?'

He nodded towards the door in brusque dismissal.

She stood up. 'But Dr Fielding——' His head was bent over a folder on the desk in front of him and he didn't look up. In acute bewilderment she walked slowly to the door but as her hand reached for the knob a loud crash behind her had her instinctively cringing against the panels, her arms protectively over her head.

Firm hands on her shaking shoulders pulled her upright and thrust her back into her chair. 'I'm sorry, my dear, that was a dirty trick to play on you, but if a glass hitting a tiled floor can provoke such an extreme reaction from you, even *you* will have to admit you're not as fit as you claim to be.'

Bethan watched mutely as he bent to clear up the shattered pieces of the tumbler he had deliberately thrown on the floor, bitterly ashamed of the shivers of shock that were making her whole body shake but powerless to stop them.

He dropped the pieces in the waste bin and straightened. 'How long is it you've been working for the agency? Six years?' And when Bethan nodded he went on, 'Six years of privation, six years of working under impossible conditions, often on barely subsistence rations and sometimes in great physical danger, witnessing the most harrowing sights imaginable, sights that would make a strong man quail. Six years without a break.'

'I've had my leaves,' Bethan shakily protested.

'Which were invariably spent in whichever country you happened to be living in. When did you last spend a leave in England?'

Bethan tried to shrug her shoulders, but they were still shaking too much to make it look convincing. 'Eighteen months, perhaps. Before I went to Beirut.'

Hugo Fielding was more familiar with Bethan's record than she was aware and he knew her last break in England had been three years ago, and then had only been a mere three weeks. He looked at the fine-boned young woman in front of him and wondered, not for the first time, at the incredible dedication and sense of purpose that had led her into the work she was doing, that was prompting her back to it now, when most young women would have considered they'd done their bit after such long service and such a close brush with death. He wondered too how she could have reached her late twenties without some man sweeping her off her feet and giving her a family of her own to dedicate her life to. The slender figure and narrow hands and feet, the entirely deceptive fragility put him in mind of a highly bred racehorse, and her heart-shaped face with the huge greenish eyes was infinitely appealing, touching the male protective instinct. If he'd been twenty years younger and not well married . . .

'And how much longer do you think you can go on without cracking up?' he demanded, his concern making his voice rougher than it should have been. 'Even if you hadn't gone through the traumatic experience of being caught in a bomb blast, I'd say it was time you took a long break. As it is you've barely recovered yet from your injuries and your nerves are shot to pieces. It's not something a fortnight's holiday is going to cure. You need at least three months' convalescence, Bethan, preferably six. And then I'd be happier if you took a less taxing job back here in Britain.'

Bethan stared at him feeling a different kind of shock. 'You're telling me the agency no longer wants to employ me?' Her mouth felt dry and she only got the question out with difficulty. This was something that hadn't occurred to her, that she would no longer be considered fit to work.

'It isn't a matter of us wanting you or not.' Dr Fielding found the stunned gaze of those large eyes disquieting. 'It's *you* I'm thinking of, my dear. You've been pouring yourself out for other people far too long. It's time you made some sort of a life of your own.'

'But it *is* my life. For the last ten years I've never

wanted to do anything else.' There was a note of
desperation in her argument that the doctor was quick
to notice. She sat forward on the edge of her chair as
she went on fiercely, 'And what about the children I've
been caring for? You talk about the hazards and
privations *I've* been working under; they have no
alternative but to face those same hazards every day of
their lives. Is someone going to suggest *they* come to
Britain for a break? And do you really think I could live
with myself if I took a safe, comfortable job here,
knowing all over the world children are *dying* for the
lack of a little skilled care?'

'I do know you have a very acute social conscience.'
The doctor was studying his hands but brought his
head up quickly to fix her with his penetrating gaze.
'I've often wondered why.'

His soft voice hit her like a blow and she flinched
visibly, the sense of guilt that was always on the
periphery of her consciousness suddenly weighing
unbearably heavy. The little girl would have been
eighteen now, blooming into womanhood, perhaps
falling in love; the same age she herself had been when she
had criminally and irresponsibly taken that young life.

'Bethan, you can't cure the ills of this benighted
world single-handed,' Dr Fielding said at last when it
became obvious she wasn't going to break her silence.
'You've done more than enough for suffering humanity
in the last six years.'

Bethan knew there were children living now who
would have died but for her nursing care. But it wasn't
enough. No matter how many young lives she had a
small hand in saving from sickness and starvation, it
would never pay off her debt, never be adequate
reparation for the life she had taken that night ten years
ago.

'But what will I do if the agency sacks me?' She
wasn't aware she had spoken aloud until the doctor said
with a touch of impatience, 'There's no question of us

sacking you, Bethan. Heaven knows we *need* nurses of your calibre. But there's no way we're going to send you on another assignment yet.' His voice hardened at the stricken look on her face. 'Surely I don't have to point out to you of all people just how much of a liability you'd be to the rest of the team while you're still in this weakened and shocked state.'

Her head bowed. 'I'm sorry,' she said huskily. 'You're right, of course. I'm afraid I was being selfish and only looking at it from my own point of view.'

'Selfish! I only wish you *would* be selfish. In fact I heartily recommend that you *do* think about yourself for once.' Dr Fielding relaxed back in his chair, returning to his usual affability now he had won his point. 'Give yourself a long break, Bethan. At least six months' convalescence, and then if you're still of the same mind and want to stay with the agency, come and see me again.'

It was something in Bethan's lost look as she rose and thanked him politely for sparing his time that prompted him to add, 'Maybe you should give me the address of where you'll be staying.' It occurred to him that as Bethan had spent so little time in Britain these last six years she might not be very close to her family, and that a word to them that a little spoiling wouldn't come amiss might be appropriate.

The big green eyes were blank. 'I'm sorry but I've no idea where it will be.'

'You've no family to take care of you?' he asked sharply.

Even as she shook her head she was thinking of her mother, still living, she supposed, somewhere in America. But even if Bethan had known where to find her, she knew she could expect no care from that quarter. To her mother she had never been anything other than a nuisance, an unwanted responsibility, and when Bethan was only thirteen her mother had happily abrogated that responsibility, leaving her daughter in the care of her adoptive stepfather while she went off to America with her lover. And since then Bethan had neither seen nor heard from her.

Her stepfather . . . Bethan closed her eyes momentarily because that could still hurt even after ten years. She had loved Charles Latimer very much, finding with him the only secure home she could ever remember, an affection her starved young heart had craved, even if his son Mark, her stepbrother, had often done his best to spoil their relationship. She had been over the moon with happiness when Charles had legally adopted her and given her the right to bear his name, Latimer, instead of her own father's name of Steele, a father she didn't remember. But she had brought disgrace to her stepfather's name. She couldn't blame him for disowning her after what she had done, but even so far distant in time the feeling of pain and loss was still sharp.

'No, I have no family,' she said dully.

'Friends?' Dr Fielding looked hopeful.

Again Bethan shook her head, smiling faintly this time. 'A few acquaintances I might look up, but no one close enough to impose myself on for six months! Don't worry, Dr Fielding, I'll ask the almoner here if she can help me find some inexpensive digs. I should have enough money to keep myself for a month or so. After that I'll have to find myself light work of some kind.'

The director of the relief agency swore so extensively that Bethan's eyes widened. 'I'm sorry,' he apologised for his colourful burst of language, 'but that *isn't* the kind of convalescence I had in mind for you. What you need is complete relaxation and freedom from worry, with plenty of gentle exercise in clean, fresh air.'

Bethan had to admit it sounded like paradise, but she smiled at him wryly. 'A large proportion of the world's population need that but have even less chance of getting it than I do,' she reminded him.

'You will,' the doctor vowed, and Bethan was startled by his vehemence. 'I've no idea how, but you will. Just leave it to me, Bethan. I'll think of something and I'll be in touch.'

That had been two days ago. Bethan turned from the bathroom mirror and began to dress, pulling on the cotton skirt and shirt she wore now she was allowed out of bed during the day. Not that she had really expected Dr Fielding to come up with anything. With the best will in the world he couldn't work miracles. She couldn't possibly afford the fees any private convalescent home he might know of would demand, and he would hardly go around asking any of his friends to take her in, even if she'd been willing to accept the charity of strangers.

Anyway, the almoner had given her the name and address of a small private hotel she could move into when the hospital discharged her tomorrow. It solved her most immediate accommodation problem, even though it left her future for the next six months highly problematical. The hotel charges for room and board, comparatively modest as they were, would run through her savings before the first month was up. As Dr Fielding had said, her life this last six years had often been hard and hazardous, but at least she had always known she had a bed to sleep in, food—though sometimes unpalatable and not very plentiful—to eat and congenial company to share her burdens. It made her feel frighteningly vulnerable to know she was on her own, that for the next six months she had to feed and house herself on pathetically small resources and at the same time build up her strength to resume her work.

Tears had actually flooded her eyes before she stiffened her backbone, despising herself for succumbing to self-pity. She began briskly to clean the bath. Once she had been discharged from the hospital she would have more than enough time on her hands to look for somewhere cheaper to live. And as soon as she had overcome this silly tendency to weep at the drop of a hat, maybe she would be able to find a part time job.

The ward was still humming when she returned to it, visitors huddled round each bed. Bethan always chose visiting times to have her bath, knowing she could have a leisurely soak without anyone battering impatiently on the door. And it made her feel less conscious that there was never anyone to rush in to sit beside *her* bed.

But today as soon as she pushed open the door the little dark-haired student nurse pounced on her. 'Miss Steele, I was just coming to find you. You have a visitor.'

'Dr Fielding!' In spite of warning herself this visit might mean nothing, Bethan couldn't help a sudden stirring of relief as the grey-haired man rose from the chair beside her empty bed.

'Why so surprised to see me?' he asked as he handed her into the chair and himself perched on the edge of the bed. 'Didn't I say I'd be in touch?'

'Yes I know, but——' Bethan flushed. 'I know my problem's very small beer compared with the ones you have to solve every day.'

'The problem of someone you care for is never trivial,' he admonished. 'And I *have* solved it. In fact you've solved a problem for me too, or at least the problem of a very dear friend of mine.'

'*I* have?' Again Bethan felt that weakening surge of relief, although she was intrigued to know what he meant.

'I've found you a job,' he said triumphantly, and Bethan's jaw sagged in astonishment.

'But—but I thought you said——' she began

'And I meant exactly what I said, but this is rather a special job. Let me explain.' He settled himself more comfortably. 'An old friend of mine, a Mrs Lorna Ruston, is due to have a replacement operation on a badly arthritic hip, but unfortunately a couple of weeks ago she caught a nasty virus infection that's pulled her down badly. What she needs is not so much nursing as

a watchdog to make sure she builds up her strength
again sufficiently to face the operation. Her nephew's
been trying to persuade her to agree to having a nurse,
but she's been very stubborn about it, refusing to have
"someone starchy fussing over her and bossing her
about" as she puts it. A very independent lady is
Lorna.' His voice was wry, but betrayed a wealth of
respect and affection for his troublesome friend.

'Well, I've been to see her,' he went on. 'I've told her
about your predicament, and frankly the idea that
you're both in the same position—that you too need to
recover your health and strength—tickles her fancy and
has removed all her prejudices about having a nurse in
the house.' He grinned complacently. 'Actually it's a
very neat solution. Your job will be to see she follows a
strict regimen; no worries, plenty of rest and good
food—a regimen you'll follow yourself, of course—
while Lorna will see herself as looking after *you*, so she
won't feel her independence is threatened. And both I
and her family can relax, knowing there's someone in
the house trained to spot any signs that she's not
responding to the building-up treatment as she should.'

It sounded too good to be true, to have companionship and a roof over her head and still feel she
was earning her keep. 'You're sure there really *is* a job
for me to do?' Bethan asked doubtfully. 'I'd be most
terribly embarrassed if I thought this friend of yours
was taking me in out of charity.'

The doctor's grey bushy eyebrows shot up towards
his receding hairline. 'You're a fine one to knock
charity, Bethan. Don't think I don't know where the
salary you could have saved to see you through an
emergency like this has gone.'

Stunned that this man appeared to know so much,
her lips parted in a gasp, then mortified colour stained
her neck and flooded into her cheeks. 'I don't see that
any small donations I might have made in the past to
help people in real need entitles me to sponge on your

friend for six months, Dr Fielding,' she said in a strangled voice.

'Sponge!' The doctor looked taken aback, as if he didn't know how the conversation had come to take this turn. 'Who said anything about you sponging? Bethan, haven't I already explained that any benefit you get out of the arrangement you'll be repaying in full by the favour you'll be doing for us? Maybe Lorna's case isn't as desperate as those you've been handling this last six years, but she *does* need you. Pain is still pain whether it's suffered in poverty or with all the trappings of luxury, and believe me, wealth doesn't protect anyone from personal tragedy. It didn't help Lorna when her husband had a massive heart attack while driving along the motorway a few years ago. She lost her husband, her only son, her daughter-in-law and her grandson that day, and sustained injuries herself to her legs and pelvis that have led to her present worsening arthritic condition. Can't you find it in your heart to feel some compassion for her?'

Bethan hung her head, feeling crushed and humbled by the doctor's disclosures. Perhaps working for so long in war-torn and famine-stricken areas of the world among people fighting for mere survival *had* led her to dismiss the needs of those more fortunate. And if she was honest she would admit her pride had revolted at the thought that this friend of Dr Fielding, a pampered and cosseted member of that more fortunate society, had been persuaded, perhaps reluctantly, into taking a waif into her home. Pride and a deep-seated conviction that she didn't warrant anyone's charity, however reluctantly given.

But the word-picture Dr Fielding had drawn erased these personal considerations from Bethan's mind. Poor Mrs Ruston, to have lost her whole family like that! Bethan knew only too well what it was to lose everyone she loved at a stroke, to know herself utterly alone, but where in her own case she had only her own criminal stupidity to blame, Lorna Ruston had been guiltless, the victim of a cruel accident. Bethan's heart went out to the unknown woman in piercing sympathy.

Her voice was husky with emotion as she said, 'I'm sorry, Dr Fielding. Of course I'll help your friend. I'll do everything I can for her for as long as she needs me.'

Dr Fielding leaned over and squeezed her clasped hands. 'Thank you, my dear. You've taken a weight off my mind.' He had been going to add, 'A double weight,' but thought better of it. It had been Bethan's warm compassion for someone in need that had prompted her co-operation and to remind her of the benefits to herself might even now upset what he saw as an ideal solution. But once again he couldn't help wondering at this fragile young woman's reluctance to think of her own comfort and well-being. He knew so little about her except that she was one of the agency's most willing and selfless nurses, and he couldn't help but be curious to know what it was that had made her the way she was.

Stifling that curiosity he said briskly, 'Now that's settled the hospital will be able to discharge you tomorrow morning, and Lorna's arranging for a car to be here to pick you up. The personal belongings you left behind you in Beirut were packed and returned to the UK, so I'll make sure they're on hand in my office first thing in the morning and the driver can collect them before he comes on here for you.'

Bethan had the breathless feeling that events were sweeping her along too fast. 'That's very kind of Mrs Ruston,' she murmured uneasily, 'but doesn't she want to interview me first? I mean, surely she'll want to assure herself that I'm the kind of person she'll be happy to take into her home? It would hardly help her to regain her health if she found she didn't like me.'

Amusement curved the doctor's mouth at the very idea that Lorna could take a dislike to this self-effacing young woman. They were rather alike in some respects,

both having a quick compassion for the helpless and
vulnerable. 'Well, in the normal course of events I
suppose her nephew would have spoken with you first,
but as he's out of the country on business at the
moment . . .' He shrugged, his smile widening. 'Not that
either of them would question my recommendation, I
think, and I'll eat my hat if you and Lorna don't take to
each other on sight.'

Bethan found herself smiling in response, her doubts
fading at his confident optimism. 'What time would you
like me to be ready?' she asked quietly, and knew that
come what may, she had committed herself to caring
for Lorna Ruston for as long as it took.

'Let's say ten-thirty, shall we?' Dr Fielding suggested.
'That'll give the driver time to collect your luggage from
my office first, so there'll be no delays to your journey.
You're bound to find it tiring, your first day out of
hospital.'

Bethan didn't doubt it and in spite of her reluctance
to accept cosseting she couldn't feel she deserved, she
couldn't help being relieved that she wouldn't have to
struggle to her destination on public transport. A
destination still unknown to her, she realised suddenly.
'You haven't told me where I'm going—where your
friend lives,' she reminded him.

Dr Fielding struck his forehead with the heel of his
hand. 'Ah—stupid of me! It's Suffolk. Deepest Suffolk.
A tiny village not far from Framlingham. I doubt if
you'll find a more beautiful house or a more peaceful
spot on the face of this earth. And whether you'll admit
it or not, it's what you need, my dear; a period of
recuperation for both body and spirit.'

At the first mention of the word Suffolk, Bethan
went very still. It was a part of the world she'd once
known well, at least an area on the Suffolk/Essex
border. A part of the world that stirred memories she
would rather not recall, a time of her life when she'd
known happiness and security, when she'd believed

herself to be facing a blissful future instead of the bitter hurt and disillusion that had culminated in the night when her safe world had been irrevocably shattered.

But Dr Fielding was still talking and she made a conscious effort to listen. After all, Framlingham was quite some way from Sudbury, wasn't it? And it was hardly likely she would meet anyone she had known in those days.

'You should arrive in time for lunch,' the doctor was saying. 'After which you will rest. And I mean that, Bethan.' He looked at her severely. 'Your own good sense should tell you you won't be the slightest use to Lorna if you're shattered. I expect *two* well people to result from this job of yours. Dr Stratton, Lorna's GP, has promised to drop in at the earliest opportunity to check you over, and——' he swept on as Bethan opened her mouth to protest, '——to give you your instructions as to Lorna's treatment. I shall expect you to co-operate with him in all things, Bethan, but I anticipate his advice will be the same as mine as far as your own recovery is concerned; no overtiring yourself and absolutely no stress.'

Bethan found herself nodding meekly, but later she was to remember his words with a sense of helpless desperation.

The nurses who had looked after her so well said goodbye to her on the ward and a porter escorted her down to the main entrance of the hospital, carrying the small bag that, together with the single suitcase the agency had been taking care of, constituted all she possessed in the world.

Stepping out of the lift into the busy entrance hall Bethan knew a moment's panic, an urge to return to the familiarity and security of the ward, but the porter was already leading the way to the reception desk and a stocky, middle-aged man in a tweed suit turned at their approach.

'Miss Steele?' he queried, and when Bethan nodded,

his round, weatherbeaten face split into a grin. 'I'm
Ernie Flowerdew. Mrs Ruston sent me to collect you.'

Bethan held out her hand, responding to his
infectious grin with a smile of her own. 'Hello, Mr
Flowerdew. It's very kind of you and Mrs Ruston to go
to so much trouble on my behalf.'

'Thass no trouble, my dearie,' he assured her in his
slow, Suffolk burr. 'Though to hear my Molly talk
thass all kind of troubles I could get *into*, spending a
night out of her sight.' His blue eyes twinkled. 'Is this
all you've got?' He took her bag from the porter, who
raised his hand in farewell and hurried away.

'Yes. That is—there's another suitcase——'

'Oh, I've got that safe and sound,' her escort assured
her. 'We'd best get away then.' He held the door for her
and led the way to a grey Rover parked nearby. 'Would
you like to sit up along o' me?' he asked when he'd
dropped her bag into the boot, and when she nodded
her agreement he handed her in and fastened the safety
belt.

'I didn't realise you'd have to stay overnight in
London because of me, Mr Flowerdew,' Bethan said as
he slid into the seat beside her. 'It must have taken you
away from more important things.'

Her companion glanced at her curiously as she spoke,
noticing her anxious embarrassment. 'Never think it,'
he assured her quickly. 'Been a nice change for me. And
thass given this ol' car a chance to stretch her legs 'stead
of puttering round the lanes. And if you're worrying
about putting us to expense, then don't. I stayed at the
boss's place. He has his own little flat here.'

Bethan had assumed Mrs Ruston was his employer
but his reference to his boss as 'he' made her wonder.
The nephew Dr Fielding had mentioned, perhaps? For
some reason she shivered in apprehension.

'You cold?' the kindly Mr Flowerdew asked at once,
and turned on the heater.

The late May sunshine was bright but there was a

distinct nip in the air that penetrated her light cotton
jacket as soon as she'd stepped outside the centrally
heated hospital. 'I've been working abroad and I'm
afraid I'm not acclimatised yet. Neither are my clothes
suitable to the vagaries of an English summer,' she
added wryly.

'And you've been ill, I believe?' He looked at her
questioningly.

'I—had an accident,' she prevaricated, unwilling to
go into details of the circumstances that had put her
into hospital. 'They—the doctors—insisted that I took
on less taxing work until I'm fit enough to go back to
my old job, hence this post looking after Mrs Ruston.
But I want to stress that I'm not an invalid, Mr
Flowerdew,' she hastened to add, 'and I don't expect
either Mrs Ruston or her staff to treat me as such. I
may not be fully fit but I'm perfectly capable of pulling
my weight.'

Ernie Flowerdew shot her another glance before
returning his full attention to the road. Not an invalid,
maybe, but she certainly looked as if the first puff of
wind would blow her away. 'Just as long as you help get
our lady on her feet again, Miss,' he said laconically.
'Knocked her back badly, that bug she caught. And the
name's Ernie, so less of the Mr Flowerdew.'

Bethan smiled, relieved by his matter-of-fact attitude.
If the rest of Mrs Ruston's household were like this
man she was going to be very content. 'Thank you—
Ernie. And my name's Bethan.'

'You don't want to be addressed as Nurse, then?'

'No. That is . . .' Doubt entered her voice. 'Not unless
Mrs Ruston prefers it that way.'

Ernie flashed her a grin. 'Right. Miss Bethan it is.'

Bethan grimaced. She hadn't been called *Miss* Bethan
since—she shut the thought off abruptly and fell silent,
aware her companion needed all his concentration to
deal with the London traffic. She didn't speak again
until they had reached the A12 when the car was able to

put on speed, and then it was only to comment on the countryside and any passing places of interest.

It was as the car swept along the Colchester by-pass and she saw the signs to Sudbury that she said involuntarily, 'It's all so changed!'

'You know this part of the world then?' Ernie glanced at her, noting the crease in her forehead that drew her winging brows together.

Bethan let out a long breath. 'Once, a long time ago. Almost another lifetime.' And because Ernie's silence was questioning, 'There was a schoolfriend I used to stay with . . .'

Ishbel Laurie. The nearest Bethan had ever come to having a sister. Popular, madcap Ishbel, impulsive to the point of recklessness and yet with a sympathy that made her fiercely protective, fiercely loyal to those who earned her friendship.

Bethan, guilty at leaving the stepfather she adored when she knew he was so hurt, almost paranoid with shame at her beautiful and utterly amoral mother's well-publicised affair with an American film actor and her departure for America with him, had found to her horror during her first few days at boarding school that her mother's misdoings were common knowledge among the girls.

It had been Ishbel who had put an end to the malicious comments, who had stilled their cruel tongues. Bethan could see her now, her single black plait swinging like an angry panther's tail, her blue eyes spitting fire as she had taken Bethan's part.

It had been holidays spent at Merrifields, Ishbel's lovely rambling home about five miles from Sudbury, that had shown Bethan the warmth and stability of family life; mother, father, uncle, aunt and a clutch of cousins all sharing the enormous, beautifully kept but still homely farmhouse. And Fraser, of course, Ishbel's elder brother.

Fraser. She hadn't allowed herself to think about him

for so long. Already a man when they had first met, twenty-two to her own very naïve thirteen years. He had teased her out of her painful shyness, comforted her when she took a toss from the little mare he was teaching her to ride, and later, when because of her friendship with Ishbel, the two families—the Lauries and the Latimers, her stepfather Charles and stepbrother Mark—had been drawn closer, Fraser had protected her from Mark's hurtful and confidence-destroying remarks.

When she had first known him she had wished fervently that Fraser could have been her brother instead of Mark, who had never accepted her, but by the time she was eighteen she had known a brotherly relationship with him was the last thing she wanted. She knew now it could only have been a girlish infatuation, but dear God! how she had loved him, with all the ardency that had been in her. And how his rejection had hurt! Yet until that terrible moment of disillusion there had been times when she had felt certain he was at last seeing her as a woman and not a child, when she had been certain he was as aware as she was of the overwhelming forces pulling them together, moments when he had kissed her, sometimes with a drugging tenderness, sometimes with a suppressed anger, as if he felt drawn to her against his will.

In her naïve infatuation she had read all the signs wrong, of course. He had only encouraged her because he had seen her friendship with his sister as a steadying influence on the volatile and easily led Ishbel. And that had been the most ironic twist of all!

Ernie overtook a juggernaut container lorry. 'A long time ago?' he queried teasingly. 'Couldn't be *that* long. What are you now, twenty-two, twenty-three?'

His voice startled her out of her painful memories. 'I'm twenty-eight, Ernie, and it *was* another lifetime.' Because that night of Ishbel's eighteenth birthday party had broken the thread. She had never seen Fraser or Ishbel again.

It had hurt dreadfully that they had followed her stepfather's lead and cut her ruthlessly out of their lives, but it was no more than she had deserved, and after ten years the hurt had blunted to acceptance. She could even wonder what they had done with their lives. They would both be long married by now, of course, perhaps with families of their own. But when she found herself wondering if Fraser had married the glossy Lisa Farraday she found the idea painful. Bethan could still remember their shared laughter, Fraser's and Lisa's, laughing at *her*, still feel the echoes of the burning humiliation that had seared her.

Silly to let it touch her now. She hadn't thought about Fraser Laurie in years, and she didn't want to think about him now. Resting her head back against the seat she shut her eyes.

'That's right, my dearie, you have a bit of a snooze.'

The car was warm now, the hum of the engine and Ernie's undemanding presence soothing. She drifted into sleep.

The car slowing to take a dog-leg bend roused her. 'We're nearly there, Miss Bethan,' Ernie said as she stirred, and sitting up she found they were following a narrow lane with high hedges either side, so narrow that to pass an oncoming car both vehicles would need to mount the verge. Rounding another bend a sign at the roadside announced the village of Nunsford, and almost at once the high hedges gave way to a straggle of cottages before the road separated to surround an irregular-shaped village green. On one side of the green were more cottages and a mellow red-brick pub, its sign depicting a vine heavy with grapes, and on the other side a small flint church with a quaint barrel tower and a large house that might once have been the vicarage but which, from the gleaming paintwork, immaculate garden and Rolls-Royce parked in the drive Bethan noticed as the car rolled slowly past, looked much too prosperous to still be the home of the minister of such a small parish. The road wandered on beyond the green, curving round the churchyard with its weathered headstones, and the car followed it, but just when Bethan thought they were leaving the village behind another cluster of buildings came into view, stone-built farm buildings, yet too clean and spruce surely to be part of a working farm, and with no evidence of livestock that she could see. The car crunched on past an entrance signposted, of all things, Visitors' Car Park, and then, beyond a stand of trees, turned off the lane into a gravelled drive. And there stood the most charming house Bethan had ever seen, a long, low house nestling under a thick thatch of Norfolk reed. Tudor, she guessed, the walls between the exposed oak frame of narrow bricks weathered to a glowing rose. The car had hardly stopped before the wide front door flew open and a woman with a mop of frizzy hair wearing a flowered overall peered anxiously out.

'That's my Molly.' Ernie grinned as he released Bethan's seat belt. 'Always expecting the worst to happen is my Molly.' As he got out of the car and came round to open Bethan's door he called across to his wife, 'Here we are, my girl, safe and sound, so you can take that fretting look off your face. This here's Miss Bethan, Molly, come to look after Mrs Lorna.' He drew Bethan forward.

'Time to fret is when I *don't* worry about you, Ernie Flowerdew,' his wife said tartly, then she smiled as she took Bethan's outstretched hand. 'Come along in now, Miss,' she urged. 'Mrs Ruston's been on thorns waiting for you. Ernie'll see to your bags.'

Bethan followed her into a wide, oak-beamed hall that ran right through the house to give a glimpse of a sunny garden through the glass doors at the far end. The floor was solid oak and smelt of beeswax while a carved-oak staircase, its shallow treads equally shining, curved away to the upper floor. The housekeeper led the way to double doors to the left of the hall and pushed them open. 'Nurse Steele's arrived, Mrs Ruston,' she said and stood back for Bethan to enter.

It was a large, comfortably furnished sitting-room, full of light in spite of the low, exposed-beam ceiling. To her left a log fire flickered cosily in the huge inglenook fireplace, but Bethan's eyes were drawn at once to the right, to the source of light that flooded everywhere. The wall between what had once been two rooms had been removed to waist height, leaving only the massive oak posts to support the upper floor, and in the further room, which she could see was a dining-area, the upper floor too had been removed so the beamed ceiling soared up to the V-shaped roof of the house. But what held her riveted gaze was the far end of the dining-room where the entire outside wall had been stripped to its ancient timber skeleton, the bricks removed and replaced with glass from the ground right up to the pointed gable.

'Oh, it's magnificent!' Bethan breathed involuntarily.

A rich chuckle had her head whipping back to the sitting-room, her dazzled eyes focusing on the elderly woman sitting in a wing-chair beside the inglenook fireplace. 'I'm so sorry. How do you do, Mrs Ruston.' Embarrassed colour touched her pale cheeks. 'You must think me very rude.'

'Not in the least.' The rich chuckle rolled out again. 'I never tire of watching people's reactions when they see this room for the first time. My husband was a very tall man and he insisted there had to be one room in the house where he could walk upright without bumping his head. Come closer, child, and let me look at you.'

It was a very long time since anyone had called her child, and Bethan smiled wryly as she obeyed, taking her own inventory as her employer surveyed her. Mrs Ruston sat very regally in her wing-chair, and her white hair drawn back in soft, smooth waves into a chignon in the nape of her neck emphasised her proud carriage. But the two elbow crutches by the side of her chair were a reminder of why Bethan was there, and the fine wool blue dress that exactly matched the older woman's eyes hung on her as if she had recently lost a lot of weight. Her face too was pale, lines of pain deeply etched, yet her eyes were bright and lively, as if her spirit refused to let her give in to her infirmities.

'You look tired. I think you'd better have your lunch on a tray in your room then go to bed for the rest of the afternoon,' she said, and Bethan stiffened.

'Please, Mrs Ruston. I know Dr Fielding doesn't consider I'm fit enough to go back to my old job yet, but I'm not an invalid. I'm here to look after *you*, and you'll make my position here impossible if you don't allow me to do so.'

Bethan caught the twitch of her lips as her employer turned her head to where the housekeeper still hovered in the doorway. 'All right, Molly, serve lunch in ten minutes.

'Well, if you won't go to bed, at least sit down before you fall down.' The sharp blue eyes were trained on Bethan again and she sank obediently into a chair. 'Hugo said you'd got more spunk than sense.' There was something like admiration if not approval in those blue eyes now. 'I hope he told *you* the last thing I need is a starchy nurse bossing me about in my own home?'

The tone of her voice didn't match the tartness of her words and Bethan found herself smiling. 'Indeed he did, Mrs Ruston. And I'll promise to be neither bossy nor starchy if you'll promise not to treat me as if *I* was the patient.'

The rich, infectious chuckle bubbled up again. 'Done. Welcome to Vine House, Bethan. I think we're going to get on very well.'

A few minutes later Molly Flowerdew wheeled in the heated trolley with their lunch, calling them to the table. Bethan stood up at once and crossed to her employer's chair. 'Is it easier for you to stand up unaided or would you like me to help?'

'If you would just give me your arm to steady me . . .'
Mrs Ruston pressed a lever on the side of her chair and
the back of the seat began to rise slowly, lifting her
forward to her feet.

'I say, that's handy!' Bethan's eyes widened in
admiration.

'You've never seen one of these chairs before? But
then I suppose that isn't so surprising. Such invaluable
aids for the disabled would hardly be common in the
parts of the world you've been working in for so long.
Now, if you would pass me my sticks, my dear.'

Bethan did as she was asked and fitted her pace to
that of her employer as they moved to the dining-table.
Molly transferred the dishes from the heated trolley to
the table and left them to help themselves to steaming
hot home-made vegetable soup followed by chicken pie
that melted in the mouth.

'That won't put any flesh on your bones.' Lorna
Ruston eyed with disfavour the small portion Bethan
had put on her plate.

'I don't have a big appetite at the best of times,'
Bethan assured her, 'and after so many weeks cooped
up in hospital . . .'

The older woman grimaced sympathetically. 'I know
illness can make eating a penance instead of a pleasure,
and Hugo told me how terribly injured you were. It
must have been a dreadful experience. I can only say
how much I admire your courage and fortitude, taking
on such difficult and dangerous work. You're the kind
heroines are made of.'

'Please, Mrs Ruston.' A long shudder shook
Bethan's too-slender frame and her fork clattered on
to her plate. If this kindly woman only knew! 'There's
nothing remotely heroic about me and I'd hate you or
anyone else to imagine there was,' she said flatly. 'In
fact I'd be grateful if you'd treat anything Dr Fielding
told you about me as confidential. As far as anyone
else is concerned, I've had an accident. I'm just an

ordinary nurse who's taken this job until I'm fit
enough to resume my regular duties. It's the truth
after all.'

Those clear-sighted blue eyes looked at her con-
sideringly and then the regal head nodded. 'Very well,
my dear, if that's what you wish.'

Bethan had been seated facing that amazing wall of
ancient timber and modern glass and saw that it looked
out to a walled garden of small beds set in a geometrical
pattern among pink gravelled walks, and to move the
subject of the conversation away from anything
personal she said, 'Isn't that an Elizabethan knot-
garden?'

Mrs Ruston obligingly followed her lead, bemoaning
the fact that she had to rely on Ernie Flowerdew to
look after it now, and as Bethan seemed to have hit on
a subject of over-riding interest to her employer she
managed to keep the conversation along these channels
for the rest of the meal.

'You're going to have your rest now, Mrs Lorna?'
Molly said when she came in to clear the table, and
something in her tone and in the light of rebellion in
Mrs Ruston's blue eyes alerted Bethan to the suspicion
that this was an often-fought battle. And hadn't Dr
Fielding warned that his friend was a very independent
lady?

But just as Bethan was preparing tactfully to add her
own urging, Lorna Ruston said submissively, 'Yes, of
course, Molly.' Levering herself up from the table she
took her sticks and walked back into the sitting-room.
'And you must rest too, Bethan. Molly will show you to
your room. I don't tackle the stairs any more than is
absolutely necessary so I make do down here. When the
weather gets warmer we can both take our naps in the
garden,' she went on as Bethan helped her to lie down
on one of the long sofas with a cushion at her head
while Molly fetched a fluffy rug.

'You've worked a small miracle already, Miss

Bethan,' Molly said a few minutes later as she led the way upstairs.

'I gather Mrs Ruston doesn't usually follow her doctor's orders so readily,' Bethan said with amusement.

'Oh, when she was really ill she did right enough, but she's a fighter.' Molly shook her head. 'I'm not saying that's a bad thing, but there's a time to fight and a time to give in gracefully. This here's Mrs Ruston's room.' Molly opened a door near the top of the stairs and showed her a spacious bedroom decorated in soft shades of blue.

'That one,' she indicated a door in a passageway to the right that Bethan realised was a gallery overlooking the dining-area below, 'is where Mr Fraser sleeps when he's here.'

It was as if a blast of cold air had hit her, stippling her skin with goose bumps. 'Mr Fraser?' she said faintly.

'Aye, Mrs Ruston's nephew,' Molly confirmed. 'Spends a lot of his time here now, to be near Miss Miles I expect. You'll be meeting her too, no doubt. A lovely young lady, even though I sometimes think he's too old for her. But then Fraser Laurie's quite a catch. And this is your room, Miss Bethan.' She opened a door at the end of a short passage to the left, unaware that her words had turned Bethan to stone.

CHAPTER TWO

THE walls of her bedroom were white, the carpet a pleasing shade of sage green while the duvet cover on the comfortable-looking double bed and the matching curtains were in a pretty flower-sprigged cotton in toning greens, giving the room a delightful freshness and femininity.

Molly indicated a door leading off. 'That's your bathroom. All the rooms have their own.' That too was in shades of green and white to match the bedroom, the pattern on the tiles exactly repeating that on the sprigged curtains.

Knowing the housekeeper would expect a response Bethan forced her stunned brain into action. 'It's beautiful, Molly. I'll have to watch I don't get soft, staying here.' She was only half joking, for the luxury was a far cry indeed from her bare room at the Beirut hospital or the many tents she had called home in the various African countries her job had taken her to.

Still feeling shocked and confused she wandered to the window protected by a beetling brow of overhanging thatch. It looked out on to the knot-garden, but now from this height she could see over the enclosing wall and blinked at the serried lines of green stretching almost as far as the eye could see down the south-facing slope. 'They can't be vines, surely!' she exclaimed.

'Indeed they are,' Molly said proudly. 'Mr Ruston planted the first lot twelve years ago and now we have about twenty acres. Produce some of the best English wines in the country, too. Not that I'm much of a wine-drinker myself,' she hastened to add. 'Now, Miss, Ernie's brought your luggage up. Would you like me to unpack for you?'

31

Bethan, longing to be on her own to pull herself together and decide what she must do, managed to raise a smile. 'Thanks, Molly, but I'm sure you've more important things to do, and as you can see, there isn't much.'

'Well if you're sure . . .' Molly retreated to the door. 'Now you do as Mrs Ruston says and rest. I'll call you when tea's ready.'

As the door closed behind the housekeeper Bethan sank down on to the edge of the bed and stared at her pathetic pile of luggage. Was it going to be worthwhile unpacking it? But if she left here, where would she go? And how would she get there anyway, when she doubted if a village the size of Nunsford had a taxi service? And if she did leave, what possible excuse could she give to Mrs Ruston, especially after that lady's kind welcome?

Why, oh *why* had fate played such an incredibly capricious trick, she wondered frantically, bringing her path back to cross that of Fraser Laurie again? She *must* be jumping to conclusions, surely she must. It would be just too much of a coincidence if Lorna Ruston's nephew really was the same man she had known all those years ago; the man she had once loved so much.

And yet in her bones she knew it was. It was unlikely there could be *two* Fraser Lauries, especially as Merrifields couldn't be more than thirty miles away from Nunsford. Visits to Merrifields over the years had made her aware that the Lauries had other business interests beside farming the land around the house, and what could be more natural than Fraser taking an interest in his aunt's vineyard after that aunt had been widowed?

The panic-stricken thoughts scurrying in circles round her head brought her to her feet again to pace the floor and finally to sink to the window seat and press her heated forehead against the cool glass. Slowly the utter

peace and quiet of the scene before her began to restore
logic and reason to her shocked mind.

Of course she couldn't just walk out of this job.
Lorna Ruston needed her. Having met her, Bethan
could see now why Dr Fielding had been so pleased
with the arrangement. A nurse fussing officiously over
her would have fretted Mrs Ruston to death, bringing
out her spirit of rebellion and having exactly the
opposite effect on her from that intended. Bethan didn't
credit herself with having worked the 'minor miracle'
Molly had commented on; it had been her patient's
compassionate nature that had prompted her to
capitulate without argument into taking her rest,
knowing Bethan herself needed to rest too. And while
she continued to believe Bethan needed looking after,
she would be easy to persuade into following her
doctor's instructions, if only to set a good example to
her nurse.

And perhaps she had panicked unnecessarily, Bethan
thought as the shock of the housekeeper's unknowing
revelation receded. It had all happened so long ago, her
infatuation and Fraser's rejection. There might be some
embarrassment when they met again but it would all be
on her side, and surely she could handle it, now she was
a mature woman? Fraser would almost certainly have
forgotten it anyway, even if finding her here in his
aunt's home reminded him of the terrible thing she had
done that had changed her way of life so radically. The
prospect of his possible displeasure at meeting her again
was something she didn't relish, but would nevertheless
have to bear.

Coming to the decision that there would be no
running away, that having committed herself to Lorna
Ruston's well-being she would have to see it through
whatever difficulties Fraser Laurie's presence presented,
Bethan began to unpack the bag she had brought with
her from the hospital, carrying her toilet things through
to the bathroom and putting her plain brush and comb

on the pretty dressing-table. Her mouth even curved in
wry amusement as she made a bet with herself that this
was the first time the dressing-table had carried so few
female fripperies. But then there'd never been any need
for make-up and perfume in the kind of life she had led.
It hadn't always been that way, of course. When she'd
been an adolescent blossoming into womanhood she
had enjoyed experimenting, revelling in the difference
clever make-up could make to her appearance and in
the effect it had on the opposite sex. She shrugged and
turned to the bed to tuck her nightdress under the
pillow. It was a long time since she had bothered about
her appearance, since she'd felt the urge to make herself
attractive to one man in particular.

She crossed back to the dressing-table to gaze at
herself in the mirror as a thought struck her. There
was always the chance that Fraser Laurie wouldn't
even recognise her! Her hair had been redder then,
distinctly carroty, the shoulder-length waves unkempt
more often than not. Years under the scorching sun
had faded the fieriness to gold and the present short,
fluffy halo was unfamiliar even to herself. Then, her
face had been childishly rounded, her figure sleekly
well fed. Now there were hollows where none had
been before, her cheek and jaw-bones sharply defined,
especially when she was tired. There was no longer
any youthful optimism shining from her eyes, either.
That had been quenched for good that terrible night
of Ishbel's party.

She doubted that even her name would jog Fraser's
memory. Bethan Steele would mean nothing to the man
who had known her as Beth Latimer, for as a child her
first name had always been shortened.

Feeling more optimistic of her ability to cope with
the unwelcome situation, she turned her attention to the
suitcase that had been sent on after her from Beirut,
hanging the thin cotton slacks and skirts and shirts in
the large wardrobe, noticing how very shabby and

faded they were after so many launderings and dryings in the fierce sun.

She found the brown paper parcel at the bottom of her case and wonderingly drew it out. Tearing the paper away she gasped as she saw the gleam of coffee-coloured silk. It was a caftan she had never seen before, embroidered at the deep V-neckline and hem with fine gold thread, and as she held it up a piece of paper fluttered to the floor. Picking it up she found it was a letter signed by all the staff of the Beirut children's hospital with the wish that she would soon be recovered enough to wear the enclosed gift. Tears blurred her vision at their generosity and thoughtfulness, and she knew she would always treasure this exquisite thing, even though she couldn't imagine when she would ever get the opportunity to wear it.

Even though her mind was still too unsettled to sleep, Bethan lay down on her bed after she had finished her unpacking until Molly called her. She found her employer better rested and after they had drunk the tea and eaten some of the delicious home-made biscuits Molly had served to them in the sitting-room, Mrs Ruston proposed a stroll in the gardens to show Bethan round. 'Though you'll need a coat, my dear. The wind's still keen even though the sun's shining.' She looked askance at Bethan's light cotton jacket.

Bethan was forced to admit she didn't have anything more substantial, explaining, 'I've spent so little time in England in recent years I never bothered to replace my old overcoat.'

'Never mind, I'm sure we'll find you something.' Mrs Ruston made her way slowly to the downstairs cloakroom where she took a sheepskin jacket from a peg. 'If you'll just help me into this . . .'

Bethan held it while she shrugged her arms into the sleeves then her employer pointed to a much larger sheepskin on the next peg. 'You can borrow that for now. It belongs to my nephew, so it'll no doubt drown you, but at least it'll keep the wind out.'

It was true, the coat reached down to her knees and her hands disappeared altogether, but it was a very fine sheepskin and surprisingly light. It was the knowledge that it belonged to Fraser Laurie that accounted for the shiver that ran through her as she drew it round her.

They strolled around the knot-garden while Mrs Ruston pointed out the different varieties of plants, and when they reached a square, brick-built summer house set into the wall on one side of the garden she slid open the door and stepped inside. Following her, Bethan saw that this was where the garden furniture and loungers were stored, and she saw too that there was a similar sliding glass door in the opposite wall. Mrs Ruston slid this open too and Bethan found herself in yet another walled garden, this one enclosing a swimming pool.

'I do hope you swim, Bethan.' The older woman looked at her hopefully.

'Well yes, but——'

'It's the one kind of exercise that seems to ease my hip,' Mrs Ruston went on before Bethan could find an excuse for her reluctance to display her scarred body in a swimsuit. 'Though of course the weather will have to get a lot warmer yet before they let me go in, even though the pool's heated.'

Bethan found herself hoping the weather would stay cold, and then felt immediately guilty, realising how very frustrating it must be for someone so obviously used to being active to find herself reduced to hobbling around on two sticks, interests like gardening and swimming denied her. 'I'll pray for a heatwave for you then.' She smiled at the white-haired but very game lady by her side, moved by a very genuine liking. What did it matter, after all, who saw her own scars?

They played chess after dinner that night, and when Bethan won easily Mrs Ruston exclaimed, 'Where did you learn to play like that? I thought I was pretty good, but you wiped the board with me.'

'Nonsense, you were the most worthy opponent I've had in a long time,' Bethan disclaimed. 'And I've had a lot of practice.' Her smile was impish. 'Out in the African bush with only a hurricane lamp for lighting, there's not much choice of leisure-time activities.'

There was curiosity about her nurse's former way of life in Lorna Ruston's blue eyes but all she said was, 'No television or discos, you mean? Well, I'll look on that as my gain. Now I know what I'm up against I demand a return game.'

She began to set the pieces out again but Bethan glanced at the businesslike watch on her wrist and saw it was already ten o'clock. 'Perhaps we've both had enough for one day, Mrs Ruston,' she suggested tactfully.

About to object, Lorna Ruston noticed the bluish bruises beneath the girl's eyes and pulled the lever on her chair to stand immediately. 'You're right, of course. My revenge will have to wait until tomorrow. Call Molly and tell her we're going up, will you, dear?'

Bethan crossed the wide hall and found her way to the kitchen at the far end of the house, and Ernie as well as Molly followed her back to the sitting-room. The reason became apparent as Ernie carefully gathered Mrs Ruston into his arms and carried her upstairs to deposit her equally gently on the edge of the bed.

'Will you be needing me tonight, Mrs Lorna?' Molly glanced at Bethan uncertainly.

But tired as she was, Bethan was determined to do the job she was being paid for. 'Perhaps you could get Mrs Ruston a hot, milky drink, Molly,' she suggested, and the housekeeper ducked her head in acquiescence.

She had her employer comfortably settled in bed by the time Molly returned with a steaming mug on a tray. 'I've left your drink in your room, Miss Bethan. It should be cool enough to drink by the time you're in bed yourself.' The tone of her voice brooked no argument, and Bethan felt unable to protest that she didn't expect Molly to wait on her.

Bethan noticed a bottle of tablets on the bedside table. She picked them up, examing the instructions on the label as she asked, 'Hadn't you better swallow a couple of these with your milk?'

Lorna Ruston flicked a hand at them dismissively. 'They're only pain killers and I only take them when necessary. I don't believe in allowing myself to become dependent on any drug.'

From the gallant little lady's pallor since she had removed her make-up and from the stiff set of her mouth, Bethan guessed her patient *was* in pain, even though she wouldn't admit it.

'You're quite right, of course,' she said craftily. 'I think it's time I stopped taking the tablets the hospital prescribed for me.' They were a mild sleeping-tablet, only meant to be taken if the nightmares that had plagued her first few weeks in hospital recurred, but she didn't see any reason to explain that.

'Do you think that's wise, Bethan?' Mrs Ruston said at once. 'If the doctor thinks you need——' She broke off, blue eyes meeting deliberately innocent green ones. *'Touché!'* she said wryly. 'You'd better pass me my dose if I'm expected to set a good example.'

Bethan couldn't help but respond to the twinkle of amusement in the blue eyes with a conspiratorial smile of her own. She had promised she wouldn't be starchy and bossy but she hadn't promised not to get her own way by other means if necessary, and what was a bit of gentle blackmail if it ensured her patient a good night's rest?

She watched while the older woman swallowed her capsules, and taking the empty glass from her, asked, 'Is there anything more I can do for you before I say good night, Mrs Ruston?'

The soft light made a shining nimbus of Bethan's red-gold hair but emphasised the hollows beneath her cheekbones. Gazing up at her, Lorna Ruston thought how extraordinary it was that she had felt so drawn to this too-slender girl right from the moment she had first walked into the house. A lot of it was sympathy and compassion for all this girl had suffered, of course, but Lorna knew it was more than that. Liking, yes, admiration too. Gentle and vulnerable she might be, but Bethan was far from weak and had courage many a man might envy.

'Yes, there is, my dear,' she said quietly in answer to the girl's question. 'I'd like you to see us as two friends helping each other, rather than nurse and patient. And I'd like you to call me Lorna.'

Unexpected tears stung Bethan's eyes. 'Thank you,' she said huskily. 'I'll be proud to have you as a friend— Lorna.' She pulled the duvet up closer round the other woman's frail shoulders. 'I'll say good night now. Sleep well.'

Lorna smiled up at her happily. 'Good night, my dear. Just make sure you get a good night's rest yourself.'

It was only as she was climbing into bed that Bethan was struck by an unpalatable thought. If Fraser Laurie recognised her and told his aunt of the guilty secret in her past, would Lorna Ruston wish she hadn't offered her friendship? Would Fraser care to come home and find his aunt's nurse on such intimate terms with her anyway? Perhaps in the morning she should suggest that she only used Lorna's first name when they were together in private.

With so many doubts and apprehensions on her mind Bethan didn't expect to sleep well, but sleep she did, deeply and dreamlessly, to be woken by the sun shafting in between the curtains and the sparrows squabbling in the thatch. After taking a quick shower she dressed, pulling on a cotton T-shirt beneath her long-sleeved cotton blouse as extra protection against the chill of the

morning and slipping her cotton jacket on top.
Brushing her short halo of hair gently because her scalp
wounds, though healed, were still tender, she wondered
what time Mrs Ruston woke.

When she found her way to the kitchen Molly looked
at her in surprise. 'My word, you're an early bird. I was
going to bring your breakfast up on a tray.'

'Oh Molly.' She smiled at the housekeeper ruefully.
'I'm just not used to being waited on, you know.
Besides, I'm here to do a job, look after Mrs Ruston.'

'That's as maybe, Miss Bethan, but you're the kind of
young lady as folks like to do things for.'

Bethan flushed in pleased surprise at the sincerity in
the other woman's voice. 'Thank you, Molly,' she said
quietly. 'Actually I came down to ask what time Mrs
Ruston likes to get up and to find out what her usual
morning routine is.'

'I usually takes her tray up at eight o'clock,' Molly
explained. 'Then she reads the papers while I get Mr
Fraser's breakfast when he's here, and after that I goes
up and helps her to bath and dress.'

Apprehension jolted Bethan at the mention of
Fraser's name but she hid it quickly. 'Yes, well, they're
the jobs I'm here to take off your hands, Molly, and if
you run this house single-handed I'm sure you won't
object to a bit of help.' She didn't want the kindly
housekeeper to feel her toes were being stepped on, but
Bethan was determined to be allowed to pull her
weight.

'Not quite single-handed, Miss.' Molly grinned at
her, showing her susceptibilities hadn't been hurt.
'There's a woman comes up from the village a couple of
days a week to clean. Even so, I'll be glad to have you
doing some of the running about, especially when Mr
Fraser's not here to help with his aunt.' Her grin faded.
'Just as long as you don't overdo things, Miss Bethan.
Mrs Lorna did say as you're only just out of hospital
yourself.'

'But quite recovered now, thank you,' Bethan said firmly. 'And believe me, looking after just one undemanding patient in a delightful home like this is a rest cure for me. So you will allow me to take Mrs Ruston her breakfast and to do the necessary for her?'

'Aye, she's taken to you too,' Molly said apropos of nothing and with a pleased twinkle. She glanced at the clock on the wall. 'Still half an hour to go before she'll want her tray, so you just go along to the dining-room and I'll bring you your breakfast first. What'll it be? Bacon and egg?'

'Oh, just toast and coffee for me, please, Molly, and some fruit juice if you have it.' She glanced round the kitchen that seemed to have every modern appliance and yet kept its cosy atmosphere and was obviously where the Flowerdews took their meals. 'And if you wouldn't mind, I'd rather like to have it in here with you.'

''Course I don't mind.' Molly took cutlery from a drawer and set a place at the big table in the middle of the room. 'And what do you say to a nice poached egg to go with the toast?'

Bethan capitulated with a smile.

She took Lorna Ruston's breakfast up at eight o'clock and stayed to chat, hoping her presence would encourage her patient to eat all Molly had so temptingly prepared, and later helped her to bath in the bathroom that had every conceivable adaptation to assist the disabled. During the morning Dr Stratton dropped in, examining his patient first and then insisting on having a look at Bethan too, firing questions at her, taking her blood pressure, examining the healed lacerations on her scalp and back and shining a light into her eyes. His instructions before he left were as Dr Fielding had predicted, plenty of good food for both of them to build up their strength, gentle exercise without overtiring themselves and absolutely no stress.

That first day set a pattern, Bethan taking over all

the duties of looking after her employer that Molly had
previously performed. Lorna made no more objections
against following her doctor's instructions to the letter,
knowing Bethan had to follow them too, and the feeling
of oneness in the gentle conspiracy drew them even
closer together, so that Bethan found herself calling her
employer Lorna when they were alone quite naturally.

Only one thing marred the healing peacefulness for
her, and that was when Lorna spoke of her nephew
Fraser with obvious affection, sometimes speaking of
Merrifields and other members of the family too.
Bethan worried whether she ought to tell Lorna that
she knew the Lauries, that years ago she had been very
close to them indeed, had looked on Merrifields as a
second home. But she knew such an admission would
bring questions from Lorna, questions like why had she
lost touch with them all so completely, which she could
only answer by uncovering her terrible guilt and
running the risk of losing the friendship she was coming
to value so highly. If Fraser recognised her and told his
aunt of her discreditable past then she would have to
bear it, but if he didn't then surely he wouldn't thank
her for claiming old acquaintance and reminding him of
a relationship they would both far rather forget? So
Bethan held her tongue.

By the fourth day when still no mention had been
made of Fraser Laurie's return to Vine House, Bethan
was beginning to tell herself she had worried for
nothing. Perhaps his visits would be so brief and
infrequent she might not even meet him.

Ernie had run them into Framlingham that
afternoon and while Lorna paid a visit to her
hairdresser, Bethan, promising herself a look at the castle
another day when she had more time at her disposal,
browsed in a second-hand bookshop she discovered on
Market Hill. Going up to her room to tidy herself
before dinner that evening she glanced again at the
battered old volume she had bought for a few pence

because the illustrations of old English houses and
gardens had appealed to her, and was thrilled to find
one of the photographs was actually of Vine House and
the knot-garden, taken before the wall between the
beams in the gable end of the dining-room had been
replaced by glass. Excitedly she carried the book with
her downstairs to show her employer.

'Lorna, look what I've f——' Her voice broke off in a
strangled gasp and the excited animation drained out of
her face as a tall, dark figure lounging on one of the
sofas rose slowly to his feet, and for Bethan time spun
in a dizzying spiral back ten years.

She would have known him anywhere, even though
his dark brown hair was cut closer to his head now and
there was a sprinkling of grey at the temples. He had
been twenty-seven when Bethan had last seen him, a
full-grown male adult, but the last ten years had given
him an added maturity, his broad shoulders keeping the
fabric of his jacket taut, the tailored trousers doing little
to disguise the length and power of his muscled legs.
His face was leaner, the indentations running from his
slightly irregular nose to the corners of his well-shaped
mouth giving him a sardonic look that hadn't been
there before, though the grey eyes she had in the past
seen reflect a whole gamut of emotions—laughter,
mockery, anger, even tenderness—were coolly blank.

'Bethan, isn't this a surprise, Fraser turning up days
before we expected him?' Lorna said excitedly from her
usual chair by the inglenook. 'But of course you two
haven't met yet, have you?' Her rich chuckle rolled out.
'You'll have guessed though, Bethan, that this is the
nephew I've been boring on about all week. Fraser,
meet my nurse and most congenial companion, Bethan
Steele.'

He held out his hand and Bethan was forced to move,
transferring the book she held to her left hand and
putting her right in his. At his touch she felt suddenly
weak and breathless, devastatingly aware of him, and in

that moment she knew he still had all the old magnetic attraction for her.

'A two-way surprise Miss—Steele.' Neither her name nor her appearance had seemed to raise a flicker of recognition and the way he had extended his hand towards her had seemed no more than the polite acknowledgment of a stranger, but that slight pause before saying her name made her wonder and she shivered. He released her hand and turned to his aunt. 'When I went away you were still dead set against the idea of having a nurse, and I come back to find one already installed.'

'It did happen rather quickly,' his aunt admitted. 'Bethan's been ill and needed a light job to give her time to recover. It was Hugo's idea that she should come to me, and I must say I'm very grateful to him for thinking of it. We get on splendidly, don't we, Bethan? Now what was it you were rushing in here to tell me, my dear?'

For a moment Bethan looked at her blankly, her senses still vibrating at Fraser's nearness, her mind still off-balance, wondering if he *did* know her and if he meant to tell his aunt. Finally pulling herself together she held out the book. 'I found this in Framlingham today and I thought you'd like to see it.' She found the right page. 'Look, there's a picture of the house taken years ago.'

Lorna gave a crow of delight as Bethan laid the book on her lap. 'Oh Fraser, do look! You must show this to Siriol; she'll be fascinated. Have you seen her since you got back, by the way?'

'Yes, I called in at the winery first to see how the bottling is going and she'd just finished showing a party around. I've asked her over for dinner if that's all right with you, Lorna?' He had glanced at the illustration in the book then directed a coldly searching look at Bethan.

'Of course it's all right. You know you don't have to

ask,' his aunt assured him. She turned to Bethan. 'Siriol Miles is Fraser's fiancée, Bethan. Her father bought the old rectory a few years ago and did it up. I'm glad she's coming tonight. I'm sure you'll like her, and she'll be some young company for you.'

So he was still unmarried then, but soon to change that. Bethan refused to recognise a sudden ache.

'Do I take it she hasn't been up to the house to see you while I've been away?' Fraser asked sharply, frowning.

Lorna suddenly looked uncomfortable. 'Not for the last few days,' she admitted. 'But the tourists are starting to arrive and she's been kept busy. Siriol helps Fraser as a guide,' she explained for Bethan's benefit, 'taking visitors around the winery and showing them what goes on. You'll have to join one of her tours while you're here, Bethan.'

'I thought Miss—Steele was here to look after you, not go junketing around the district.' Again there was that unnerving hesitation as Fraser said her name, and his implication that she would be prepared to neglect her patient for her own enjoyment made her smart at the unfairness.

But before she could defend herself Lorna said sharply, 'Don't be silly, Fraser. Bethan's entitled to some free time.'

'You might feel like taking a gentle stroll over to the winery yourself one day if it's not too far,' Bethan said placatingly, not wishing to become a bone of contention between aunt and nephew. Fraser's attitude to her made her deeply uneasy. Surely if he *had* recognised her he would have said something by now? But if he hadn't, then why was he so hostile? After all, both Dr Fielding and Lorna herself had said he had been keen to engage a nurse for his aunt.

But there was no more time to wonder. There was the sound of the front door opening and closing and light footsteps crossing the hall. A petite girl with shoulder-

length black hair and thickly fringed dark eyes burst
into the room.

'Siriol, my dear!' Lorna smiled a welcome.

The girl went at once to Fraser, linking her arm in his
and hardly able to tear her eyes away from him to say,
'Hello, Aunt Lorna. Isn't it marvellous to have Fraser
home early?'

'Hello, sweetheart.' There was no coldness in Fraser's
grey eyes now as he looked down at the girl hanging on
his arm. 'I understand you haven't met the new
addition to the household yet, Lorna's—nurse, Bethan
Steele.' Again there was that almost imperceptible
hesitation that kept Bethan on tenterhooks. 'Miss
Steele, this is my fiancée, Siriol Miles.' There was an
unreadable expression in his eyes as he made the
introduction.

Bethan's first reaction was one of shock. *This* was his
fiancée? But she looked so young, no more than twenty,
barely more than half Fraser's age. And it was
something rather more than shock she had to admit to.
There was a sharp pain too, deep down, and with
dismay she recognised it as jealousy. Ten years ago
Fraser Laurie had rejected her, leaving her in no doubt
that he had no place for her in his life, and after all
those years it was still painful to meet the girl who was
to be his wife.

But aware of Fraser's sardonic eyes watching her,
Bethan hid both the shock and the betraying jealousy.
'I'm very happy to meet you, Miss Miles,' she said
quietly.

'Oh Siriol, please.' The other girl's smile was warm
and friendly 'And I'll call you Bethan. It's such a pretty
name, don't you think so, darling?'

'I used to like it once.' Fraser's voice, like the
expression in his eyes, was flat and hard, but when
Siriol looked up at him in surprise his face relaxed. 'As
you say, it's a pretty name,' he agreed indifferently.

Lorna showed Bethan's book with the old illustration

of Vine House to Siriol and the tension eased as they fell to discussing when the photograph might have been taken, but all the time Bethan was acutely aware of Fraser, and aware that his eyes often rested on her with cold speculation. It was a relief when Molly came in with the loaded dinner-trolley and Bethan jumped up to help Lorna from her chair and into the dining-area.

'I'm glad to see you take your duties seriously, Miss Steele,' Fraser said as she lowered Lorna carefully into her chair at the table. There was a sardonic twist to his mouth that belied his apparently innocuous remark.

'Indeed she does!' Lorna Ruston answered for her, smiling at her fondly. 'Hugo was quite right when he predicted she would suit me very well. But don't let her gentle manner deceive you, Fraser. Bethan has her own way of keeping me in order and persuading me to do as I should.'

Fraser took his own chair when he had seen Bethan seated and for some reason she realised he was furiously angry, and yet his question, 'You know Hugo well, Miss Steele?' sounded reasonable enough.

'I can't say I know Dr Fielding well, but we've been acquainted for quite a few years now,' she replied quietly. 'I've been working abroad for too long to be able to say I know anyone in England well.'

'But he obviously felt he knew *you* well enough to recommend you for this job,' Fraser said silkily. 'Do you do much private nursing?'

Bethan toyed with her soup-spoon, her appetite deserting her under his questioning because she couldn't help feeling there was some hidden purpose behind it. 'No, this is the first time.'

His dark eyebrows lifted. 'So what made you change your habits? Oh yes, you said something about having been ill and needing a less arduous job.'

'Darling, do you *have* to fire questions at the poor girl all through dinner?' Siriol laughingly protested. 'You're not giving her a chance to eat.'

Fraser stood up to pour out the wine, which Bethan refused with her hand over her glass, and he didn't look pleased at his fiancée's protest. 'Surely it's only natural I should want to know something of Miss Steele's background and qualifications,' he retorted stiffly. 'That *is* what you said, isn't it, Miss Steele?'

'I—I had an accident.' Bethan glanced at Lorna, silently begging her not to enlarge on her bald statement. Fraser was already so hostile, she was sure if he was given a full explanation he would see it only as a bid to ingratiate herself.

'What kind of accident?' he pressed.

Bethan shifted uncomfortably in her chair and shot another pleading glance at Lorna, who was frowning. 'A—a street accident,' she said, knowing her face was flooding with guilty colour.

'You walked in front of a car?' he was openly disbelieving. 'And this happened in London, I suppose.'

'No, I've already told you I was abroad.'

'Oh yes, so you said. America, wasn't it? So why come back to England for medical treatment?'

'America!' She couldn't imagine why he should think that. 'No, it wasn't in America. And my—my employers had me brought back to London.'

'Your—employers? Now who would *they* be?' He was like a cat pouncing on a mouse, Bethan thought wildly.

But this time it didn't need another pleading glance to bring Lorna to her rescue. 'That's quite enough, Fraser,' his aunt said firmly. 'Can't you see Bethan doesn't wish to talk about her accident?'

She began to talk to Siriol about the stage the wine-bottling had reached and under cover of their conversation Fraser said to Bethan in a low voice, 'Oh yes, I can see all right, and I'm sure I don't need two guesses to know *why* you're so reluctant to talk about it.'

Bethan's startled and apprehensive green eyes clashed

with his hard grey ones. But at least Lorna had put an end to his questioning if not to her own frantic wondering. What on earth had he meant by that last remark? *Had* Fraser recognised her as the girl he had known and rejected all those years ago, the girl who had brought disgrace to her stepfather's name? She could think of no other explanation for his barely concealed antagonism.

The meal seemed to stretch on interminably, but though Bethan took little part in the conversation she had ample opportunity to study the man she had once been infatuated with. Because that was all it had been, she told herself distractedly. And this skin-prickling awareness of him she felt now was nothing more than the lingering threads of that infatuation, that and his all-too-obvious dislike of finding her in his home.

Ten years ago there had been a certain arrogance about him at times, but not the cynical hardness, the ruthlessness she sensed now. There was no way she could imagine *this* man finding time to coax a shy teenager out of her shell as the younger Fraser had. Even his face was all hard lines as if hewn from granite. She couldn't imagine the man he had become showing kindness, let alone tenderness. And yet Siriol Miles loved him. Bethan only had to see the way she looked at him, the way she touched him to know that. And what did he feel about the girl who was his fiancée, she wondered. He must feel *something*, she supposed, or he wouldn't have asked her to be his wife. But he displayed few symptoms of a man in love. His attitude to Siriol seemed to be little more than a tolerant affection. Or was it perhaps that a man such as he didn't care to display his emotions? Maybe alone with Siriol he was very different. For just a moment she allowed herself to remember what it had been like to be in his arms, then slammed the shutters of her memory decisively.

The meal did eventually come to an end and Bethan began to stack the dirty plates on the trolley as the others moved back to the sitting-room to take their coffee.

'Don't you bother with them now, Miss Bethan,' Molly protested. 'You go and sit yourself down and relax. That trip to Framlingham must've taken it out of you.'

Bethan was aware of the sardonic twist to Fraser's mouth but thought it best not to argue. As she passed by him to take a vacant chair he said in a jibing undertone, 'More junketing, Miss Steele?'

'Your aunt wanted to go to the hairdressers,' she said defensively. 'As I'm supposed to be looking after her, naturally I went along too.'

He merely shrugged and went to sit by Siriol on one of the sofas, and soon the two were in deep discussion about events at the winery since he had been away. Bethan still hadn't got over her surprise at finding a vineyard in the heart of the English countryside and would have found it interesting to listen and learn something about what went into turning grapes into wine. But Lorna said with a laugh, 'If those two are going to talk business all night, you and I will have to make do with the chessboard again, Bethan, for our entertainment.'

Bethan went to the cupboard to get the board out, thinking Fraser hadn't heard, but almost at once he said derisively, 'Chess!'

'Perhaps you'd like to take Bethan on, Fraser,' his aunt suggested. 'I promise you'll find her a very worthy opponent. I haven't managed to beat her yet.'

The thought of sitting across a chessboard with him put Bethan in a panic and it was with considerable relief she heard him say, 'I think not, Lorna.' He turned to Siriol, pulling her to her feet. 'I'll run you home, darling. I know it's early yet but I need to see your father anyway. He'll expect a report on the deal I struck with Herr Langer.'

They walked across the room together, his arm

around her shoulders, but at the door he turned. 'Please don't keep my aunt up too late, Miss Steele. And when you've seen her to bed I'd like you to wait for me in my study. There are things we need to discuss.'

'But won't it do in the morning, Fraser?' Lorna protested. 'Bethan needs her rest as much as I do, if not more.'

'No, it will *not* wait till morning.' The rigid line of his jaw betrayed his annoyance. 'There are matters about her employment here that need to be straightened out without delay. I'm sure Miss Steele understands.' The look he directed at her defied her to argue.

Had he recognised her? She was almost sure of it now. And though she was grateful that the forthcoming interview with him was to be conducted in private, she was equally sure it wasn't going to be a pleasant experience.

CHAPTER THREE

'THAT nephew of mine is in a funny mood tonight,' Lorna said thoughtfully after he and Siriol had left. 'I hope he didn't upset you, Bethan. I've never known him quite so——' she paused, searching for the right word, '—astringent with a guest before. I don't know what got into him.'

But Bethan was sure *she* knew, and her hands were not quite steady as she set out the chessmen. If Fraser had recognised her, the fact that he hadn't acknowledged it must mean he still had no wish for either himself or his family to be associated with her. Indeed, his barely concealed hostility made it clear how much he objected to finding her installed in his aunt's home, and no doubt the interview he had demanded with her was to tell her that.

'But I'm not a guest,' she pointed out. 'I'm an employee.'

'Then he has even less excuse for upsetting you,' Lorna said sharply.

That evening Bethan gave Lorna her first taste of victory, her tension making it impossible for her to keep her mind on the game, and by the time she had seen her patient to bed she felt quite sick with apprehension. But it didn't occur to her to disobey Fraser's order.

She came downstairs reluctantly only to find the study empty, but she had been told to wait for him there so she switched on the light and looked around her. Molly had pointed the door out to her earlier in the week, but this was the first time she had been inside. It was a very masculine room, book-lined, with an enormous desk and several leather-upholstered chairs in front of the empty fireplace. She perched uneasily on the edge of one of these chairs.

Twenty minutes dragged past, every one of them seeming a lifetime as she worried over the outcome of this interview. If only she had been completely open from the start, if she had told Lorna she had known the Lauries when she had first discovered who her nephew was! If only she had greeted Fraser as an old acquaintance instead of pretending tonight had been their first meeting. Perhaps if she had she wouldn't be feeling so guiltily vulnerable now. But it was no good wishing, it was too late to do anything about it. She just wished he would come so she could get it over.

And yet it wasn't just apprehension that made her heart beat faster when at last she heard the rattle of the door handle. Springing to her feet she turned tremblingly to face him.

He paused in the doorway, a strangely arrested expression on his face, and again it felt to Bethan as if time had whirled back ten years, leaving her dizzy. Then even as she watched, his expression hardened, his grey eyes impaling her like rapier-pointed icicles. Closing the door with a deliberate movement he leaned back against it. 'And now, *Beth Latimer*, perhaps you'll tell me what you're doing here masquerading under a false name and pretending to be a nurse.'

That he *had* recognised her didn't shock her; she had been almost sure the recognition was there beneath his pointed jibes. It was the savagery of his accusation that made her gasp. 'I'm *not* masquerading under a false name,' she denied indignantly. 'Steele was the name I was born with, and I reverted to it ten years ago.'

'Ah, yes, when you kicked over the traces.' His lip curled contemptuously. 'Reverted to more than your former name, didn't you? Reverted to type too. I suppose we should all have realised that under all that wide-eyed innocence you were still your mother's daughter.'

A sick guilt rose up in her. She wasn't like her mother—she wasn't! All right, maybe that one night ten years ago, getting drunk and losing all sense of responsibility ... But she had never touched alcohol since, had done her best to pay for that one dreadful aberration.

The shocked repudiation in her face only seemed to infuriate him further. He pushed away from the door and advanced on her menacingly. 'My God, Bethan, don't you *care* that you broke Charles Latimer's heart, running out on him like that? He loved you, whatever you'd done.'

Bethan fell back a step, her eyes wide with stunned bewilderment. 'I—I don't know what you mean. I didn't run out on my stepfather.'

'What else would you call it?' His contempt lashed her. 'Refusing to see him, to go back to your home. Taking off for America instead to your bitch of a mother, without caring what it would do to him.'

'To my *mother!*' She shook her head at him incredulously, unable to believe she was hearing right. 'Whatever gave you that idea? I've never been to America in my life, and you must know I've neither seen nor heard from my mother since I was thirteen years old.'

But Fraser seemed not to hear her denial or even register her incredulity. 'The only decent thing she ever did for you was to give you a loving stepfather, but you couldn't wait to fling his love and concern back at him, could you? Oh, I can understand you being ashamed to face him after your drunken accident, but to turn your back on him, on everyone who cared for you to opt for the sleazy life your mother lives—oh yes, we've heard all about your goings-on. Your stepbrother was only too happy to spread any discreditable gossip about you.'

Bethan felt as if she had entered some fantasy world. Why was Fraser making such an unjust accusation? Surely he didn't believe what he was saying? The man who had once known her better than anyone else in the world? But he seemed so sure of himself, and so utterly condemning that he couldn't have made it up. Her mind whirled as she tried to think where he could have got hold of such an improbable idea, unless—she blanched. Unless that was the story her stepfather had put out to explain her disappearance! Oh, surely not. Mark, she suspected, might be capable of such a thing but not *Charles*. She couldn't bear to think he had come to hate her so much he would spread such a story.

She wanted to shout, 'It isn't true, none of it. It was Charles Latimer who threw *me* out.' But she found she couldn't do it. When Charles had instructed Mark to tell her he didn't want to see her again, perhaps he believed she *would* try to find her mother. But then Mark had known she had done no such thing. Wouldn't he have told his father she had been accepted for nursing training by a London hospital? He *had* promised to try to persuade his father to relent towards her.

Bethan shook her head in confusion. Whether her stepfather had known what she was doing or not, he must have felt himself justified in telling everyone she had gone to her mother in America. Did she really have the right to call him a liar now, even to protect herself? Hadn't she done enough damage to his name ten years ago?

'How could I have gone to my mother when I had no idea where to find her?' she prevaricated. 'I doubt if I'd even recognise her now.'

'There are ways and means of tracking people down if you're determined enough. And I didn't have any difficulty in recognising *you*, Bethan,' he jeered. 'Did you really think I wouldn't?' He was standing very close now, towering over her like some accusing, vengeful god, and she couldn't retreat further with the desk at her back. The sheer aggression of his dark shadowed jaw intimidated her, the antagonism oozing from every pore making her tremble. No one had ever looked at her with such scorn before, and that it should be Fraser Laurie doing so now hurt unbearably.

'So let's stop the play-acting, shall we?' His hands gripped her shoulders, his fingers digging painfully into her still-tender back. 'We both know you're not a nurse. What I *don't* know is why you're pretending you are. Why have you turned up in England again, Bethan? And why here in particular? Just what are you up to?'

'I'm *not* pretending! I *am* a nurse.' Tears of pain at his punishing grip and frustration at his unjustified suspicions swam in her eyes, making them gleam like emeralds. 'I've been a nurse for the last ten years,' she insisted, her mouth trembling.

He couldn't seem to take his eyes off that trembling mouth, so unknowingly inviting, and for the first time a flicker of uncertainty crossed his face as the tension between them tightened so that neither of them seemed able to move.

Bethan's heart seemed to skip a beat and then accelerate its pace and crazily she wanted to touch him, to trace the planes of his face that she had never entirely forgotten. 'Fraser . . .' she breathed.

Instantly the uncertainty was gone to be replaced by a cold savagery. 'A nurse? When I know you haven't an ounce of compassion in your body? You'll be claiming next that it's pure coincidence that you turned up here.' He pushed her away from him in disgust and she lurched backwards across the desk.

Levering herself upright Bethan knew she was near to collapse, her weakened state allowing no reserves to combat her emotional turmoil, especially in the face of Fraser's blank refusal to believe a word she said. Her face paper-white, her head bowed, she said dully, 'I can't *make* you believe me, but it's true all the same. I'm an experienced nurse and when I took this job I had no idea Mrs Ruston was related to you. If I *had* known, nothing would have induced me to come here.'

'As you say, you can't make me believe you, and I

don't.' His voice was cold but his hands tightened on the back of one of the leather chairs, betraying his anger. 'Get out of my sight, you lying little bitch. Go on, get out before I do something I might be sorry for.'

For several frozen seconds Bethan stared at him, then on shaking legs she fled from the room. Somehow she made it up the stairs to her bedroom and flung herself on the bed, too shocked and hurt to cry, feeling as weak and drained as ever she had in hospital.

It had been a day of shocks, first the unexpected meeting with Fraser when she had almost made herself believe that meeting was going to be postponed indefinitely, then seeing him with the woman he intended to marry and realising she was still as powerfully attracted to him as she had been all those years ago. And now this implacable hostility, his scathing condemnation of what he believed her to be, some scheming little tramp.

She still found it unbelievable and deeply hurtful that her stepfather should have told such an untrue version of what had happened, that he should have deliberately turned everyone against her to save his own face. It was so out of character. Perhaps when he had sent her away he hadn't trusted her to *stay* away. But surely he must have known she would do nothing to embarrass him further? Had he really found it necessary to tell everyone she had just disappeared, run out on him, gone to join her mother in America? That was such an unlikely story to have told when he knew very well her mother wouldn't have welcomed her. After all, she thought bitterly, her mother had had little enough time for her even before she had deserted them both to run off to America with her film-star lover.

And yet Charles Latimer *must* have told such a story or Fraser wouldn't be so sure of himself, so contemptuously ready to call her a liar. He seemed convinced her arrival at Vine House had been deliberately planned for some devious purpose of her

own, though what he thought she meant to do, or even
why she should want to do anything, she couldn't
imagine.

Lying in the darkened room staring blindly up at the
ceiling, Bethan told herself it shouldn't matter what
Fraser thought of her. But it *did*. It mattered very
much. His indifferent rejection of her love ten years ago
had lacerated her, but his distrust—even hatred—of her
now seemed to shrivel her very soul. It was as well he
had told her to go or she might have been tempted to
clear herself in his eyes. And that was something she
couldn't do, for to tell the truth, that it was her
stepfather who had thrown her out and not she who
had deserted him, would show the man to whom she
owed so much to be a liar.

Somehow she found the strength to drag herself off
the bed and to begin to pack, Fraser's bitter, 'Go on,
get out of my sight,' ringing inside her head. She had
no idea where she could go. Perhaps the pub in the
village would put her up for the night, and maybe
they could find a taxi for her in the morning to take
her to the nearest railway station. Where she would
go from there she neither knew nor cared, as long as
it was as far from Vine House and Fraser Laurie as
possible. It meant she would have to leave without
saying goodbye to Lorna and she deeply regretted
that, but no doubt Fraser would find some acceptable
explanation.

She should have known the contentment of the last
few days was too good to be true, she thought as she
thrust her belongings haphazardly into her suitcase.
Not until now, when she was leaving, did she admit to
herself how much she had needed the period of
convalescence Dr Fielding had insisted on, how much
she had gained from the peaceful way of life at Vine
House, from the friendship of people like Lorna Ruston
and the Flowerdews. Closing her suitcase she slipped
on her jacket, her face wet with tears. She wiped them

away with the back of her hand and left the room, closing the door behind her and walking quietly along the passageway.

She had just reached the bend in the stairs when the study door in the hall below opened. Shocked into immobility—because she had assumed Fraser had gone to bed—Bethan faltered to a swaying halt. At dinner and also during her traumatic interview with him in his study, he had been wearing a formal dark suit, but now he had taken the jacket off and the thin cotton shirt was stretched across his powerful shoulders and chest, and that brought back forcefully the few moments when he had held her powerless in the grip of his strong, hurtful hands.

His face darkened as she hesitated, his cold grey eyes raking her, taking in the shabby cotton jacket and the suitcase dragging at her arm. 'And where the hell do you think you're going?' His voice was quiet but no less menacing for that.

Bethan gathered her remaining strength and came on down the rest of the stairs. After all, he couldn't hurt her any more, could he? 'Does it matter?' she said tiredly. 'You told me to go, so I'm going. I haven't said goodbye to your aunt—I didn't want to disturb her—but I'm sure I can leave it to you to explain why you no longer want me in the house.'

He strode across the hall, snatching the bag out of her hand. 'I meant you to get out of the room, not out of the house,' he ground out. 'What are you trying to do, make me out as callous as you are, turning you out at this time of night?'

She wanted to protest that she'd never done a consciously callous act in her life but tension and near exhaustion had her bowing her head and saying defeatedly, 'Very well, I'll wait till morning.'

She reached to take her bag back from him, but he held on to it.

'It's in character, I suppose,' he bit out. 'Running

when the going gets tough. But you're not getting away with it this time.'

As he obviously didn't mean to relinquish his grip on her suitcase Bethan drew back a pace. She just couldn't think straight when he was so near, so aware was she of his intimidating masculinity; the spicy scent of the soap—or was it the aftershave?—he used, the sheer size of him, six feet of bone and muscle to her own skinny five feet four—and the fierce antagonism that kept coming at her in waves. In fact she didn't seem able to make her mind work at all, for he seemed to be talking in riddles.

'I don't understand what you want,' she muttered.

'That makes two of us, because I'd give a lot to know what it is *you* want, *Bethan Latimer Steele*, but I promise you I mean to find out before I let you leave here.' He started for the stairs, taking her suitcase with him, and Bethan had no alternative but to follow.

'And there's one thing I can promise *you*——' she began, but Fraser hushed her with a movement of his hand, hissing, 'Keep your voice down, for God's sake. Do you want to wake my aunt?'

He marched straight into her room and dumped the suitcase on the bed. 'Well, Bethan, what is it you can promise me?'

'That you're wasting your time. I want *nothing* from either you or your aunt,' she said wearily.

'Still keeping up the fiction that you're just a harmless working girl? Well, maybe it's a fiction we ought to encourage in public, for Lorna's sake. It might do you good, at that, to actually have to *work* instead of living off others.' His long arms snaked out, his hands gripping the tender flesh of her upper arms, pulling her close until his implacable face was only inches away. 'You contrived this situation, Bethan, cheating your way into this house, worming your way into my aunt's affections. Oh yes, it hasn't gone unnoticed that she's become very fond of you in a ridiculously short space of time. And she's usually such a good judge of character too,' he added insultingly. 'But then you've had ten years to polish up the winning ways you practised on me when you were a child. So, much as I'd like you out of this house, I'm not going to risk upsetting Lorna. I'm not even going to ask you how you managed to persuade Hugo Fielding to recommend you for the job of looking after her. The damage is done now. It'll do her more harm than good to know the truth about you. But let me tell you this, *Miss Steele*.' He dragged her even closer until the outline of his hard body was imprinted on her own. 'You hurt Lorna and you'll wish you'd never been born!'

Her heart was pounding thunderously against her ribs and she could hear the rushing of her blood in her ears. Her face was dead white beneath the red-gold aureole of her hair, her green eyes wide as she gazed up at him with an unconscious plea for mercy.

'God! You still look like an innocent child.' His mouth twisted with an expression that in any other circumstances she might have taken for pain. 'But we both know you're not.' He thrust her away from him, flinging her back on to the bed where she fell like a rag doll. 'How many men have you had, Bethan, since I nearly gave in to temptation and took you myself? How many men have tasted the delights of your delectable but rotten little body in the last ten years?' He loomed over her like some terrible condemning judge and fear blocked her throat, making it impossible for her to deny his shattering accusation or to say a word in her own defence, because for several terrifying moments she was afraid he was going to use her as the kind of woman he had accused her of being.

But then he turned abruptly on his heel and strode to the door. 'You can stop acting like a virgin facing rape,' he jeered, turning to look at her where she still lay unmoving on the bed. 'I have no intention of falling into your predatory little hands. So whatever your motive for insinuating yourself with Aunt Lorna, just forget it. You were hired to do a job and I'm going to see that you do it impeccably, and believe me, I'll be watching you every step of the way.'

The door closed behind him but it was several minutes before Bethan could find the strength to drag herself off the bed. She undid her suitcase and took out her nightdress, pushing the bag into the wardrobe to unpack again later. Undressing, she pulled the nightdress over her head and crawled back into bed, her mind empty, as if, like a shell-shock victim, it had taken more than it could handle and had cut off out of self-defence. Exhaustion claimed her and she fell into a deep pit of unconsciousness.

But in the morning when she woke it was to instant awareness, with no protective numbness to block out the memory of the things Fraser had said to her the night before. The two terrible scenes replayed themselves over in her mind in all their shocking detail. Fraser believed the story her stepfather and stepbrother had told to explain her absence after her trial ten years ago—that she had walked out on her adoptive father, the man to whom she owed so much, had allowed him to pay the swingeing fine the court had imposed on her conviction for drunken driving and then had uncaringly deserted him as her mother had before her, that she had taken herself off to America to be with her mother and apparently to abandon herself to a life of depravity, moving on from lover to lover. It was almost funny! Almost. She bit her bottom lip to stop its trembling.

And yet, believing all that of her, he was insisting that she stayed on here in his aunt's home. Bethan shivered. Weeks—months perhaps—of that suspicion and hostility beating her down, and she unable to defend herself against it. 'Absolutely no stress,' Dr Fielding and Lorna's GP had said. For a few moments hysteria threatened to get the better of her before she

fought it down. Little did they know that the stress
couldn't have been much greater if they had sent her
back to Beirut!

A hot shower did little to lessen the tension that
gripped her at the thought of facing Fraser again. She
unpacked the suitcase she had packed so hurriedly the
night before and dressed in a pair of washed-out cotton
trousers and shirt before going reluctantly downstairs
to the kitchen. Perhaps Fraser would be working by
now and she wouldn't have to see him until this
evening, she thought hopefully.

But that hope was dashed when she found him at the
kitchen table eating his breakfast. 'Good morning,
Nurse Steele.'

Molly Flowerdew raised her eyebrows at his
formality and the coldness in his voice, but she was
standing behind him at the stove and didn't see the
derision in the grey eyes that raked Bethan's shabbily
dressed figure. 'Very workmanlike,' he jibed, but his
tone implied, 'But you don't convince *me*.'

He looked very workmanlike himself in denim jeans
and a short-sleeved sweat-shirt, but Bethan didn't
comment on it. Her quiet, 'Good morning,' en-
compassed them both, and when Molly suggested she
might like a poached egg for her breakfast she shook
her head quickly, asking instead for toast, knowing she
would be hard put to it to eat even that in Fraser's
condemning presence, and ignoring the housekeeper's
protest. But she was very much aware of his sardonic
expression as Molly fussed over her, and although he
made no more cutting remarks she was almost limp
with relief when he stood up with a sarcastic, 'Well,
some of us have to work,' and made for the back door.

'What's up with him?' Molly wanted to know when
the door had closed behind him. 'You upset him or
something?'

'You could say that.' Bethan wondered what the
kindly housekeeper would say if she knew he believed

her to be a lying little tart who had never done a day's work in her life but lived off her many lovers. 'I think he's a bit put out because I was engaged while he was away and he didn't get a chance to vet me first.' She suggested the most likely excuse that came to mind.

Molly didn't look convinced, but said no more as she prepared her mistress's tray.

Bethan made the same excuse when Lorna asked her what Fraser had wanted to talk to her about the night before, knowing her patient would undoubtedly be upset if she told her the truth. She managed to make light of the interview and Lorna soon forgot about it as they discussed what they would do that day.

The lines of pain etched into the older woman's face spoke of a restless night, and to ensure Lorna didn't overtax herself Bethan suggested a gentle stroll in the knot-garden where she encouraged her patient to talk about the different flowers and herbs that grew there. Later she drew up two loungers in the shelter of the summer-house looking out on to the swimming-pool and there they had their coffee, staying until it was time for lunch, a meal which Fraser did not come in to share, much to Bethan's relief.

When she had tucked Lorna into a rug on one of the sofas in the sitting-room for her afternoon nap, Bethan stretched out on the other one for her own rest, a habit she had formed over the last few days rather than going up to her room. But today she felt too tense to sleep, too restless to lie still and yet too reluctant to disturb Lorna to risk leaving the room. So, half an hour later, the sound of a car pulling into the drive followed swiftly by an imperative rat-tat on the door came as a welcome diversion.

There was barely time to whisk away the rugs and for Lorna to pat her hair into place before Molly was showing in the callers, three friends of Lorna's who had come in hopes of a game of bridge. At Lorna's bright-eyed look of anticipation Bethan didn't have the heart to put any obstacles in her way, and set up the card table for them.

'But what about you, Bethan?' Lorna said suddenly as one of her three cronies began to shuffle the cards. 'Perhaps you'd like to take a turn?'

'I'm afraid my accomplishments only run to chess,' she smiled. 'If it's all right with you, I think I'll go for a walk.'

'Why don't you stroll down to the winery?' Lorna suggested at once. 'I'm sure you'll find it interesting, and if Siriol's busy you can tag on to one of her tours.'

Bethan agreed it would be a good opportunity for her to see what went on in the making of the wine, though with some reservations which she kept to herself. If Fraser was anywhere about, she wouldn't go near the place.

But there was no sign of him as she approached cautiously, leaving the house by the front door and walking along the lane to follow the signs to the visitor's car park. There were several cars there, and as she drew nearer a three-sided building, the fourth side open to the elements, one group of people was just emerging while another waited to be shown round.

Siriol appeared behind the crowd that was leaving and greeted Bethan with a warm smile. 'Hi! What a lovely surprise. Come to see where all the work's done? Hang on a minute. I'll just dish out the tickets for this lot and you can join us.'

Bethan watched as Siriol took the tourists' entrance fees, smiling and chatting a welcome. She was a very pretty girl with a natural, easy way with her, a fact that was appreciated by two young men in the party. She wore a casual but expensive outfit of trousers and waistcoat in a fine red wool over a white rollneck sweater, and for all she was so young, she handled her tourists confidently, showing no shyness. Bethan could well appreciate what an asset she must be to the business, and why Fraser had chosen her to be his wife despite the disparity in their ages. She was very conscious of her own shabby plainness beside the younger girl, and that was strange because she didn't usually spare a thought for her appearance. Perhaps it was that, if she were honest, she envied the other girl from the bottom of her heart. Siriol had Fraser's love. She was going to be his wife. Ten years ago Bethan would have given her soul to be in that position. Even now——

She brought that thought to an abrupt halt. Marriage and a family were not for her.

She was glad to turn her thoughts back to Siriol who was telling her audience the grapes grown in the vineyard were the Muller Thurgau variety which had been found to be best suited to the English climate. She indicated a gleaming stainless-steel trailer drawn up at one side of the open-fronted room. 'That's the grape-trailer,' she explained, 'and it holds two tons of grapes.'

'Why stainless steel?' someone asked. 'It must cost a bomb.'

'Because the last thing we want is to poison our customers,' Siriol grinned, 'which is what would happen if the grape-juice or wine came into contact with iron. So we use only stainless steel, enamel, fibreglass, plastic or glass equipment.'

'And when do you harvest the grapes?' someone else wanted to know.

'Usually about mid-October. We have to wait for the grapes to reach the right sugar-content before they're picked. The sweeter the grapes, the higher the quality of the wine.' She leaned into the grape-trailer and pointed out a large stainless-steel screw running along the bottom. 'The auger there carries the grapes into the berry-mill here behind the trailer. This has to split the skin of every grape without damaging the pips or stalks, or the tannin would make the wine bitter. From the berry-mill the crushed fruit is pumped into the press.'

She moved on to the next shining piece of equipment

and by now Bethan found herself fascinated. This was again stainless steel, a large drum with a panel removed to show the inner workings, a large disc at each end which Siriol explained gradually moved in towards the centre while the drum rotated, slowly squeezing the juice out of the fruit. 'We usually do about twenty-five pressings on each load of grapes,' she went on, 'by which time the pulp is bone dry, and this—known as pomace—goes back on to the vineyard as mulch.

'Now we'll move on into the winery.' She led them through a side door into a long, barnlike building, scrupulously clean with whitewashed walls and enormous fibre-glass vats ranged all down one side, stopping beside the first vat. 'Before we start to make the wine we fill the vat with carbon dioxide; this keeps the air away from the juice and prevents oxidisation. As the juice is pumped in from the press, the carbon dioxide is forced out of the vat through that valve at the top.

'When the vat is full and any imbalances in the juice have been corrected, the juice is allowed to settle before it's pumped into a clean vat and the actual wine-making begins. We use a starter wine here to begin fermentation, as the wild yeasts in the new grape juice won't make good wine.

'And this is the point where H.M. Customs and Excise take an interest in us.' Siriol grimaced. 'They collect duty on every single litre we make, so every litre has to be accounted for. *And* it has to be paid before we sell a single bottle.'

'How long does the fermentation last?' one of the young men wanted to know.

'We try to regulate the temperature in here so it lasts two to three weeks,' Siriol answered. 'When it stops the wine is pumped into another clean vat filled first with nitrogen, again to prevent oxidisation. Any minor corrections the chemists' report suggests are made then, before the wine is filtered.'

'And then you leave it to mature?' Bethan asked, full of admiration at Siriol's knowledge and very much aware of how closely the girl identified herself with her fiancé's business.

Siriol smiled at her. 'Yes, for five or six months. We do the bottling in April or May.' She trooped them all down to the far end of the building. 'Last week this was a hive of industry, but we finished bottling last year's wine only yesterday.' She went on to point out the wine-filter—a curious, concertina-like instrument—the bottle-steriliser, bottle-filler, corker and labelling machine, showing them one of the corks they used that must, by law, have the registered name of the winery branded into it. And lastly she demonstrated the machine that put the lead capsule over the neck of the bottle before leading the way out to a small inner courtyard where vines grew around the walls and white tables and chairs were set out in the sunshine, and here they were invited to taste the wine.

Bethan smilingly refused when Siriol offered her a glass. 'Don't you like wine?' the other girl asked in surprise. 'I noticed you didn't drink any at dinner last night.'

'I know it must sound sacrilegious to you, but I can't say I care for it,' she said lightly. She had drunk the occasional glass of wine in her teens but had never liked anything stronger, which made it all the more incomprehensible how she should have drunk herself into a stupor on the night of Ishbel's party. In any case, she hadn't touched anything remotely alcoholic since.

'But even if I don't care for the wine, I was fascinated by your description of how it's made,' she hastened to add. 'And I'm open-mouthed with admiration at your knowledge.'

'If *you* had to rattle it off six times a day, *you'd* know something about it too,' Siriol grinned.

'That might seem a bit like hard work for Miss Steele,' a voice behind them said and Bethan's heart

sank like a stone. Why on earth hadn't she gone back to
the house as soon as the tour was over? Why had she
been stupid enough to hang around here for Fraser to
catch her away from her duties?

But Siriol's reaction to her fiancé's appearance was
predictably different from Bethan's. Her face lit up.
'Darling!' She turned her face up and Bethan had to
watch while he kissed her inviting mouth. 'But what an
unkind thing to say,' she pouted. 'I'm not quite sure
who he's getting at, Bethan, you or me. I'm darned
certain nursing's a lot harder work than tripping out my
piece for the visitors.' Her head turned as some of those
visitors moved towards the doorway off the courtyard
marked SHOP. 'Sorry, I'll have to dash. Now they've
tasted the wine, they want to buy—I hope!' Giving
Fraser's arm a final squeeze she hurried into the shop
after her customers.

Bethan too turned to leave but Fraser caught her
arm, holding her back. 'So you didn't heed my warning.
The first chance you get you abandon my aunt to come
snooping down here.'

His grip on her arm hurt but it was his touch that
disturbed her the most. 'I didn't abandon your aunt. It
was on her suggestion I came to see the winery.' It took
considerable effort to keep her voice level. 'Some
friends arrived and I left her playing bridge. However,
I'm sure it's time I was going back now.' She tried to
detach his grip.

But he held on to her easily. 'If Lorna's playing
bridge then she won't thank you for disturbing her yet,'
he said surprisingly. 'So in the meantime I'm sure you
won't object if I find you another job to do to earn
your keep.' He dragged her across the courtyard to a
gate that led out into the vineyard, pausing only at a
tool-store to pick up a hoe.

The rows of vines were planted about eight feet
apart, each vine about four feet from its neighbour,
trained on to wires supported by stout posts. They were

some way down the long rows before Fraser stopped and thrust the hoe into her hands.

'The one job there's no end to at this time of year—keeping the weeds down round the vines. And don't bother to remind me about your supposed "accident". I'm sure it's as fictitious as your nursing experience, to make sure you won't be called upon to do anything too strenuous. Well, I'm calling your bluff. It won't do you any harm to learn what it's like to actually *work* for your living.' He turned on his heel and left her staring helplessly after him.

She could hear voices in the distance and guessed there were other workers out there somewhere but she couldn't see them, and even if she could, how would they be able to help her? She began to work, pushing out of her mind Dr Fielding's warning that on no account was she to get overtired. Fraser wouldn't have believed her anyway, and she had her pride. She would show him she wasn't afraid of work.

It was a simple enough job, loosening the weeds and leaving them on top of the ground to shrivel and die, but very soon her back and arms were aching and her hands, softened by the weeks in hospital, began to smart as blisters formed. Sheltered as the vineyard was on its south-facing slope, the sun beat down on her bare head until it swam, and perspiration trickled down her back and between her breasts.

She lost all count of time, moving like a robot as she kept doggedly on, her body one huge ache, her muscles screaming protestingly. There was only the row of vines stretching into the distance so far her glazed eyes couldn't see the end. Only her will kept her going, the determination not to give in, and she didn't even see the sun beginning to sink behind the trees or notice there were no more voices calling to each other.

It wasn't until a heavy hand descended on her shoulder and she was whirled round to stare into Fraser's furious face that the pounding in her head and the weakness of her body overcame her will. Her last thought was, 'Now he'll have one more thing to score against me,' as she slid into unconsciousness at his feet.

CHAPTER FOUR

AT first he thought she was faking to gain his sympathy. Angrily he reached down and shook her, but she didn't move. Her greenish pallor, her flaccid limpness convinced him the faint was genuine and a sickening fear punched him below the belt. Swearing, he gathered her up into his arms.

It was about a quarter of a mile back to the house but she felt no weight at all, her bones as frail as a bird's, only a tiny pulse fluttering at her temple to show she was still alive. How did she manage to look so innocent and childlike? he thought savagely, looking down at the thick, gold-tipped lashes fanning against her bloodless cheeks, her rusty-gold head pressed against his chest.

The shock had been like a kick in the gut when she'd walked into Lorna's sitting-room yesterday; thinner, although she'd always been delicately built; different with her hair cut short instead of lying in a fiery cloud on her shoulders, but he'd known her instantly and it was like being caught in a timeslip, the fingers of that old obsession clutching at him again.

In God's name! why had she come here, disturbing his peace of mind when it had taken years to get her out of his system? Hadn't she wrought enough havoc ten years ago?

He'd watched her grow from a sweet, appealing kid to a highly desirable young woman, not exactly pretty but with a heart-jerking vulnerability that got under the skin, and with a delicate bone structure that promised true beauty at full maturity.

Even at sixteen or seventeen he'd sensed in her the capacity for passion beneath her shy coltishness, and the first time he had kissed her that passion had burst into flame with an urgency that had shaken and delighted him. And like a fool he had believed it was a response she felt for him alone.

That evening of Ishbel's eighteenth birthday party when Bethan had enticed him into the summer-house at Merrifields should have warned him she was her mother's daughter and not as sweetly innocent as she appeared. He could have taken her then without protest, and might well have done had not Lisa Farraday's fortunate appearance reminded him he had a more urgent priority.

More fortunate than he'd realised at the time while he was still burning for Bethan's pearly-white body, for when the task he'd set himself had been more easily accomplished than he'd expected and he'd got back to England after his sudden trip to Australia, it was to find Bethan had already begun to show that instability that was a legacy from her mother.

His lips tightened grimly as he remembered his stunned incredulity when he'd heard that Bethan was up on a charge of manslaughter. At first he'd been convinced there was some terrible mistake, until they'd told him the facts, that at Ishbel's party she had drunk herself out of her mind, had taken her brother's car without his permission and had killed a child in her mindless progress. Even then, when his first shock at something that seemed so uncharacteristic had subsided, he'd felt pity for her and a deep concern, believing he knew what the knowledge that she had taken a life would do to a girl as sensitive as Bethan. But he'd been wrong about that too. Bethan's sensitivity had been only in his own imagination. If she could show so little concern for the man who had been the only father she had known, how could she care about some child who was a stranger to her?

God, but she'd got off lightly! Merely a conviction for drunken driving because her defence had pleaded that the child had contributed to its own death by being out at that time of night on a bicycle without lights. All it had cost Bethan was her driving licence—Charles Latimer had paid her heavy fine—and in return she had laid on him a death sentence, for a few days before her trial the stepfather she had professed to love so much had had a massive stroke. But neither before the trial nor after when she had walked free from the court had she once been to see him. Instead, not caring if he was alive or dead, she had taken off for America to her bitch of a mother, and a way of life that sickened him even to think about it if only half of what had been gossiped about her at the time was true. Fraser only hoped Charles never heard any of the stories, for he had survived—though only half alive—for another four years. He specially hoped and prayed Mark Latimer's drunken boast that he'd had Bethan himself more than once hadn't come to Charles's ears. It had taken Fraser a very long time to get over that particular piece of information himself.

But he *had* got over it. He'd cut himself off from the social circle that had once included Bethan so he didn't have to listen to any more stories of her flitting from lover to lover like her mother, had worked like a slave to drive out the disillusion, and in the process had improved the Laurie holdings out of all recognition. He hadn't lacked for female company but had made sure his relationships with women were of the fleetingly casual variety.

It was only recently he'd felt the need for something more permanent, the need to delegate some of his responsibilities and settle in one place, the need for a home and family of his own. He still hadn't finally decided where that home would be but he *had* chosen the wife who would share it. Siriol was ideally suitable. The only child of an industrialist, she was wealthy enough in her own right not to be merely attracted by his money. She was young enough to be malleable but sophisticated enough not to expect him to dance attendance on her like some love-sick calf. His life was mapped out the way he wanted it to go and he was damned if he'd let Bethan Latimer's sudden, unwelcome reappearance disturb things.

Angrily he shouldered open the back door of Vine House and faced the accusing looks of the two women hovering in the kitchen.

'She's hurt!' Molly Flowerdew stepped forward to brush back the sweat-dampened tendrils of hair clinging to Bethan's paper-white forehead.

'She's only fainted,' Fraser said tersely.

'But what happened? Where was she?' Lorna demanded. When dinner time was approaching and Bethan still hadn't returned from the winery she had sent Fraser in search of her.

A dull flush stained Fraser's cheekbones. 'I set her to work in the vineyard this afternoon. She was still there.'

Both women stared at him in horrified disbelief. 'Fraser, you didn't! Are you mad?' He had never seen his aunt so angry. 'Get her up to her room at once. Molly, call Dr Stratton and tell him what's happened, then come upstairs and help me to undress her.'

Wordlessly Fraser carried his burden across the hall and up the stairs, wanting to be irritated by the women's panic but deeply uneasy himself at Bethan's continuing unconsciousness. He laid her on the bed and stood looking down at her, feeling unaccustomedly helpless as he willed her to come round.

'Whatever possessed you, Fraser?' His aunt's voice behind him startled him, the fact that she had struggled up the stairs unaided a measure of her anxiety. 'Dr Stratton specifically said she was not to get overtired.'

'She really is recovering from an accident then?' He pushed his hands distractedly through his dark hair. 'I thought that was just an excuse so she wouldn't be asked to do much work.'

Lorna stared at him in angry bewilderment. 'Why on

earth should you think that? I don't understand you, Fraser. I've never known you to take a dislike on sight to anyone before—and for no reason that I can see.'

It was on the tip of his tongue to tell her all he knew of Bethan Latimer, the girl she was defending so staunchly, but instead he said, 'You have to admit she was very evasive when I asked her about this so-called accident last night.'

'And that was enough to make you assume——' Lorna sighed and limped across the room to sink tiredly on the edge of the bed. 'Maybe she *was* foolish to play it down like that, but that's Bethan. She didn't want it known what had actually happened to her, but Hugo told me what a very close brush with death she'd had. And he trusted me to look after her!' She glared at her favourite nephew accusingly. 'If Hugo can forgive you for this, I don't know if *I* can. What that bomb-blast failed to do, it seems *you're* well on the way to accomplishing.'

Fraser stared at her, anger and disbelief fighting a losing battle against her certainty, but before he could say a word, Molly bustled breathlessly into the room. 'Dr Stratton's just finished his evening surgery and says he'll be right over.'

Lorna levered herself to her feet. 'Perhaps you'll leave us now, Fraser. We must get Bethan into bed.'

Biting back the questions that seethed in his mind, Fraser glanced once more at the still, white-faced figure on the bed before walking out of the room that seemed to have no imprint on it of the girl who had occupied it for the best part of a week. Either Bethan had taken his aunt in completely, or there were things he ought to know. Running downstairs he made for his study. It was time he did what he ought to have done the moment Bethan Latimer Steele walked back into his life. Picking up the telephone, he dialled Hugo Fielding's number.

*   *   *

The little mare broke into a gallop and Bethan shouted aloud in joy, her long hair streaming behind her like a fiery banner beneath her hard hat, the wind hot in her face. So drunk on the triumph of outstripping Fraser was she that she never saw the rabbit hole, and the next moment she was sailing over Marinka's head and crashing to the turf. Her head felt light and muzzy as if it didn't belong to her and she hurt everywhere, but Fraser's arms were around her and she knew she was safe. She wanted him to hold her like this for ever and ever. She wanted to tell him so but something seemed to have happened to her tongue. It worried her, not being able to speak, because if she didn't tell Fraser how much she wanted him to go on holding her he might let her go.

And then the arms about her were suddenly gone and there was no more safety anywhere. She was alone, roaming the face of the earth, searching ... searching ... the cold streets of London, the burning African bush, the shattered, war-torn Middle East. She could sense again the tension that never relaxed, the fear that was a familiar taste in her mouth. The street with its bullet and bomb-scarred buildings was busy but it was a tense, uneasy busyness, with everyone hurrying as they were themselves, to do what had to be done before seeking a precarious refuge again. She heard the whine of the shell and grasped her companion's arm, felt the terror as they cringed together, looking behind them, saw the building heave a split second before the terrible blast threw them bodily forward. She screamed ...

Hard hands gripped her shoulders and forced her back against the pillows. She opened dazed, fear-crazed eyes to see Fraser Laurie's grim face staring down at her and for a moment thought she was still in the grip of the nightmare.

'It's all right, Bethan. You were having a bad dream.' The hard hands released her and he stepped back.

She remembered then, the long hours working in the

vineyard, her determination to show Fraser he was wrong about her, that she wasn't afraid of hard work, his furious arrival and her humiliating collapse at his feet. Mortified colour flooded her cheeks. What must he think of her now, lying here like a lady of leisure?

'I'm sorry,' she gasped. 'It was stupid of me to pass out like that. What time is it? Lorna——' She tried to sit up, to swing her legs out of bed but found she could hardly move, was certainly too weak to resist when once again Fraser pushed her back against the pillows.

'Don't worry about Lorna, she's safely tucked up in bed. You've been unconscious for hours. It's nearly morning now.'

'Nearly morning!' Bethan registered the soft light of her bedside lamp. 'But what are you——?'

'Someone had to stay with you,' he said curtly. 'At least until you regained consciousness.'

His tone implied he would have done as much for a dog and stung Bethan into betraying a trace of bitterness as she retorted, 'I'm sure it went against the grain when that duty fell to you, but as you can see, I'm perfectly all right now and can only apologise for being such a nuisance.'

'It was the least I could do,' he said distantly, 'when it was I who was responsible for your collapse.' He turned away towards the window, pulling the curtain aside to stare out into the darkness.

If that was meant to be an apology, Bethan thought, it was hardly a gracious one. But then he surprised her when, without turning round, he said savagely, 'For God's sake, Bethan! Why weren't you honest with me? Why didn't you tell me the true circumstances behind your arrival here? I could have done you irreparable damage, over-straining you like that.'

She stared at his rigid back incredulously, a slow anger beginning to burn in her. 'I have never, *ever*, told you anything but the truth,' she asserted vehemently. 'I told you I was a fully trained nurse. I also told you I'd taken on the job of looking after your aunt while I recuperated after an accident, but you chose to disbelieve me on both counts, obviously preferring your own lurid version of the kind of life I've been leading for the last ten years.'

She saw his hand gripping the curtain tighten, bunching the material and putting a strain on the hook holding it to the rail. 'All right, I disbelieved you, but for so long now——' He bit off what he had been going to say and dropping the curtain, turned to face her. 'But did you have to go on making a fool of me when you could so easily have *proved* you were telling the truth?'

Bethan sighed and closed her eyes, trying to decide what he was accusing her of now. 'Would you mind telling me how I was supposed to do that,' she questioned tiredly, 'when you weren't prepared to believe anything I said?'

'By suggesting I check your credentials with Hugo Fielding, of course,' he said impatiently. 'So why didn't you?'

It would have been the logical thing to do, she conceded to herself. So why hadn't she? She sighed again. Because in defending her own position she would have exposed her stepfather's version of what had happened after her trial as false, and she hadn't been prepared to do that.

A baffled look passed across Fraser's face but he pressed on. 'And then there was your evasiveness about your previous job and the exact nature of your supposed accident. You can't blame me for being suspicious. You may claim to have been honest with me, Bethan, but you weren't completely honest, were you? If you had been you wouldn't be lying there now looking like a ghost.'

She closed her eyes. Truth to tell she *felt* like a ghost, her limbs heavy and lethargic and her head light, barely in touch with reality, as if she were floating out of her body. 'I don't blame you for anything,' she said tiredly. 'I readily admit I brought everything on myself.'

The violence of the oath he swore had her eyelids
flying up again in apprehension. 'So why didn't you tell
me the whole truth?' he demanded. 'That you've been
working for Hugo Fielding's International Relief
Agency for the last six years? That you're one of his
most selfless and dedicated nurses—his words, not
mine—that you've worked for the agency in all the
trouble-spots of the world, risking your life time and
time again? That your so called "accident" was actually
being caught in a shell-blast in the fighting in Beirut?
My aunt knew all this, so why was *I* kept in ignorance?'
He had moved close to the bed again and was standing
over her, threateningly Bethan felt, and instinctively she
flinched away from him.

He had either persuaded Lorna to tell him the full
story or he had got it from Dr Fielding, but knowing
the truth didn't seem to have made his antagonism any
less. She could *feel* the leashed anger in him still, and it
tightened her own tension unbearably.

'I don't *know* . . . I was here to do a job—look after
your aunt—and I just wanted to get on with it without
any fuss.' She turned her head away to hide the tears
that were squeezing between her tightly closed lids,
despising herself for the weakness that gripped her. But
he had already seen them.

'Oh God! I didn't mean to make you cry. I shouldn't
be making you talk like this either. Dr Stratton says
you're suffering from complete exhaustion and must
rest.' Something soft brushed her face and she was
startled to realise he was wiping her tears away with his
own handkerchief. 'Is there anything I can get you
before I leave you to sleep?'

Her mouth was dry, but she didn't have the strength
to lift her head off the pillow. 'If I could just have a
drink of water.' Her eyes flicked up at him warily,
distrusting the softer note of his voice that sounded
almost kind.

He poured water from the carafe at her bedside into a

glass and one strong arm lifting her easily from the
pillows, held it for her to drink. She didn't know
whether it was her own weakness or Fraser's closeness
that made her teeth rattle against the glass, she only
knew she found his gentle touch profoundly disturbing.
It wasn't until she tried to hold the glass herself that she
noticed the bandages.

Frowning at them in puzzlement she demanded,
'What's the matter with my hands?'

'They were rubbed raw by the hoe,' Fraser said
tightly, seeing again the bleeding, broken blisters. 'Are
you in pain?'

Bethan shook her head. Even if she had been she
wouldn't have told him, for that leashed anger was
back, obliterating his momentary kindness. In fact she
felt numb from head to toe, the weight of her limbs
pressing her against the bed. Her heavy eyelids closed as
her head fell back against the pillow and within seconds
she was asleep and unaware of the man who continued
to stare down at her, a mixture of anger and
compassion in his face.

The sparrows squabbling in the thatch woke her as they
did every morning. She glanced at the pretty clock that
matched the lamp on her bedside table and saw it was
nearly eight o'clock. She'd overslept! In a few minutes
Lorna would be expecting her breakfast. It took a
tremendous effort to throw back the duvet and swing
her legs out of bed, and when she tried to stand they felt
like jelly, the room swinging crazily round her.
Grabbing the chair Fraser had been sitting in the night
before to steady herself, she waited for the dizziness and
the accompanying nausea to subside.

'What the hell are you doing out of bed?' Fraser's
furious voice from the doorway demanded.

'Lorna——' she began, then thought she saw his face
tighten at the familiarity, though it was hard to be sure
because his overpowering figure seemed to be wavering

about. 'Mrs Ruston,' she corrected herself. 'I'm late——'

'Molly can see to my aunt today, and for as long as necessary. Dr Stratton said you were to stay in bed until you were fully recovered.' Before she could argue he had swept her off her feet and dumped her back beneath the duvet.

She began to protest but he cut her off with a savage, 'For pity's sake, you crazy woman! You'll do as you're told.'

Hot colour flooded her cheeks and she would have been afraid to make another effort had the need not been so pressing. 'But I need to go to the bathroom,' she said in a small voice.

Incredibly, a dark red crept over his cheekbones and he looked suddenly uncertain. 'I'll fetch Molly,' he said and turned on his heel.

Molly clucked round her like a mother hen, brushing aside her protests at the trouble she was causing, coaxing her into eating the breakfast she had prepared on a tray. That Fraser Laurie's credit had gone down in her estimation, she made obvious before she left to see to her mistress.

And this worried Bethan. She had been speaking the truth the night before when she had told Fraser she didn't blame him for her collapse. It was hardly his fault if he had believed her stepfather's version of her disappearance ten years ago, and the fact that she *hadn't* given him a full account of how she came to be in his aunt's house must have made him feel his suspicions of her motives were justified. So it was the last thing she wanted, to know she was the cause of ill-feeling between Fraser and his family.

Her discomfort was even greater later on when Lorna came to sit with her. 'You're still very pale, my dear.' The older woman leaned over to kiss her cheek, the sharp blue eyes concerned. 'I can't apologise enough that this should have happened while you were in my house. I just don't understand what got into Fraser, but I'm going to find it very hard to forgive him.'

'Oh please, you mustn't say that,' Bethan protested in dismay. She had no idea what explanation Fraser had given for taking her away from her nursing duties to work in the vineyard, but she knew she had to do something to heal the breach in his relations with his aunt. She could see nothing for it but to tell the truth as she should have done at the beginning, even if it did mean losing Lorna Ruston's friendship and respect.

'I'm afraid your nephew has very good reason for thinking badly of me—as you will too when you know.' She looked down at her bandaged hands lying idly in her lap, not wanting to see the shock and revulsion on her kindly employer's face. 'Ten years ago I did something so utterly unforgivable ...' She bit her lip then went on purposefully, 'I got drunk at a party, took someone's car without permission, and while I was driving it, I—I killed a child.'

The silence stretched out but still Bethan couldn't bring herself to raise her eyes.

'And Fraser knows about this?' Lorna Ruston's voice betrayed only surprise and Bethan nodded miserably, believing the other woman too well-mannered to show her real feelings.

'It was at his sister's eighteenth birthday party that I got drunk,' she confessed in a whisper. 'Ishbel and I had been friends all through school and I was often at Merrifields during the holidays—my stepfather was a diplomat and often out of the country—so I used to know Fraser quite well.'

'*You're* Beth Latimer?' This time Lorna's shock was unmistakable, and to Bethan's sensitive ear had an accusing ring.

'Yes,' she choked. 'I'm sorry. Please believe I never intended any deception. Steele was my real father's name and I went back to it after—after—it didn't seem fair, you see, to go on using my stepfather's name after

I'd brought such disgrace to him. And when I agreed to come here I had no idea you were in any way connected. Of course as soon as I first heard Fraser's name mentioned I realise now I should have told you he wouldn't welcome me here in your home, but I—I thought perhaps he wouldn't remember me. I *hoped* he wouldn't. And then when he came home and didn't appear to know me, well, I didn't think he would care to be reminded.' Her voice trailed away and she steeled herself to meet her employer's distaste.

'But he obviously *did* recognise you, and apparently set out to give you a hard time.' Lorna's voice was grim. 'What I *don't* understand is why he should bear you such a grudge! He's not normally so intolerant, neither is he usually so lacking in imagination that he can't appreciate how heavily such a burden must weigh on the conscience of a girl like you.'

Bethan was startled into raising her eyes to the blue ones regarding her with compassion instead of the distaste she expected. 'You—you're very forgiving,' she choked. 'I—I thought——'

'You thought what you've just told me would make a difference to the affection I have for you? My dear child, give me credit for a little humanity. I'd say you've spent the last ten years trying to make reparation for that one fatal mistake. Would I be right?'

Bethan nodded, warmed by the other woman's understanding and yet feeling wretchedly that she didn't deserve it. Her stepfather's rejection, Fraser and Ishbel Laurie's abrupt disappearance from her life, had many years ago reinforced her own conviction that what she had done on the night of Ishbel's party was so utterly unforgivable she had forfeited the right to any understanding for herself, to any sympathy or respect.

'What I still don't understand is Fraser's attitude,' Lorna went on, frowning. 'Why he feels he must go on punishing you for what after all was a most unfortunate accident, and so long ago too.'

Lorna's charitable view of the crime she had committed brought tears to Bethan's eyes as she turned her head away. 'He—he couldn't believe my arrival here was no more than an unhappy accident,' she explained thickly. 'He seems to think I inveigled my way in here to take advantage of you—or him—for some devious purpose of my own. He certainly doesn't consider I'm a suitable person to be looking after you.' Not for anything could she bring herself to tell Lorna of the disreputable lifestyle Fraser had believed her to be living.

'Oh, doesn't he! Well, I'll soon put him right about *that*!' Lorna said grimly.

Bethan pushed herself up from her pillows in dismay. The only reason she had made her confession had been to try to heal the disruption her presence here had caused, and instead it seemed to have had quite the opposite effect. 'Oh, please Mrs Ruston—Lorna. I don't want to cause any more trouble. You must see it would be much better for everyone if we just let the whole thing drop, if I just left quietly without any more being said.'

'Leave! You most certainly will *not* leave.' Lorna was outraged. 'You're here on *my* invitation and here you'll stay until both I and Hugo Fielding consider you fully fit again.'

'But Fraser——' Bethan protested.

'You just leave Fraser to me, and no more arguments.' Lorna hauled herself painfully to her feet. 'Just you forget his stupid prejudices and rest.'

In the face of such determination, and feeling drained physically and emotionally by her confession, Bethan had no alternative but to lie weakly back against her pillows, healing sleep creeping up on her almost as soon as the door closed behind Lorna.

She slept for the rest of that day and most of the next, waking only for meals, and by the time she had made a good dinner on the evening of the third day she

was feeling much stronger, strong enough anyway to
get to the bathroom unaided and to feel wide awake
for the first time since her collapse. So when there
was a tap on her door and Siriol put her head round
to ask if she was feeling well enough to receive a
visitor, she welcomed her eagerly, only to have a
wave of weakness return when Fraser followed his
fiancée into the room.

He was wearing a light-green safari suit, impeccably
tailored in a light drill fabric, open at the neck as it was
such a warm night to show the beginnings of the dark
hair on his chest, and she watched him as he crossed the
room to sit on the window seat. 'You're feeling better?'
His voice was clipped and the expression in the grey
eyes trained on her was unreadable.

Bethan moistened her dry lips, glad of her high-
necked cotton nightdress that was anything but
glamorous. 'Th-thank you. Much better.'

'Fraser says you knocked yourself up working in the
vineyard.' Siriol's voice brought her head round sharply
to where the girl had taken a chair beside her bed.
'Whatever made you do that? I know you were
interested in the wine-making, but wasn't hoeing the
vines carrying an interest too far?'

At once Bethan's eyes swung back warily to Fraser as
she wondered how she should answer, but he was
gazing out of the window and offered her no clue. It
was obvious he hadn't told his fiancée he had *ordered*
her to work in the vineyard, and for some reason she
found herself unwilling to tell Siriol that either. So she
shrugged the question off with a light, 'You could say
that', and felt a measure of satisfaction in the startled
movement of his head as it jerked round towards her.

Siriol gurgled with laughter. 'Oh Bethan, you're cool!
But then I suppose you have to be.'

'Do I?' Bethan raised her eyebrows in surprise.

'Well I mean . . . being one of Hugo Fielding's nurses.
I understand you've been working for the relief agency

for years?' Siriol was sitting forward in her chair eagerly, her dark eyes avid with curiosity.

'Yes, for quite some time,' Bethan agreed reluctantly, hoping her uncommunicative answer would deter the girl from any more questions.

It was a vain hope, 'Oh, do tell me about it,' the younger girl pleaded. 'You must lead a very exciting life.'

'There's nothing exciting about watching sick and starving children die and being able to do little to prevent it,' Bethan said sharply, and then regretted her sharpness when Siriol looked abashed.

'No, of course not. I'm sorry. It's just that—well, the kind of life you've led makes mine seem very dull and ordinary. What countries have you worked in, Bethan?'

Ordinary? When she was loved by Fraser? Bethan thought, recognising her own envy. When she was going to be his wife, was perhaps already his lover? She shook her head to chase the unpalatable thought away. 'Oh, several African countries—Angola, Ethiopia——'

'Ethiopia?' Siriol broke in excitedly. 'Isn't that where some doctors and nurses were kidnapped by the rebels? I saw something about it on television.'

It wasn't that she really minded answering Siriol's curious questions, but all the time Bethan was uncomfortably aware of the silent figure listening on the window seat. 'Yes,' she said quietly. 'One of them was a friend of mine, though I was in the Lebanon at the time and didn't know anything about it till it was all over.'

Siriol's dark eyes were round with awe, making her seem very young. 'That's where you were injured, wasn't it, in the fighting in Beirut?' She shuddered. 'I don't know how you have the courage to take on such dangerous work. You must be very brave.'

Bethan's hands clenched until the pain reminded her of her blistered palms. 'That's utter rubbish.' She shook her head in vehement denial. 'You couldn't be more wrong. The most familiar taste to me is the metallic

taste of fear in my mouth. I've often been *sick* with
terror, wanting only to run to the nearest bolt-hole.
Once, during the siege of Beirut when we were getting
the children—all mentally or physically handicapped—
down to the shelter during a raid, I lost one of them, a
little boy, who'd wandered off into the compound not
realising the danger he was in. I had to *force* myself to
go after him, and then I was so terrified I could only do
it crawling on my hands and knees. Believe me, I'm the
biggest coward alive.'

'And yet you went back there,' a harsh voice said
from the window, and Bethan's head jerked round in
startled surprise, so immersed in remembered terrors
she had for several minutes forgotten his presence. 'To
admit your fears and yet to be prepared to face those
same fears again and again hardly smacks of
cowardice.'

Stunned and embarrassed by what was almost an
accolade, her gaze locked with his.

'Well, I know *I* couldn't do it.' Siriol's unashamed
candour defused the tension that had leapt up to
crackle between them and Fraser looked away.

'Neither you could, sweetheart. You're much too
fond of your creature comforts.' There was no censure
in his voice and the smiling affection in the look he
directed at his fiancée made Bethan close her eyes
instinctively.

Mistaking the reason for her withdrawal, Fraser rose
to his feet. 'I think Bethan's had enough of us now,
darling,' he said quietly. 'We must let her rest.'

But somehow when they had gone rest seemed very
far away and peace of mind elusive. Talking about her
life in the service of the relief agency had reminded her
that soon she would have to return to it, to the heat and
dirt and privations, to the heartbreaking sights and the
ever-present dangers. Even now the fear reached out to
clutch at her, making her shake, and she was ashamed
of being so afraid.

Lucky, lucky Siriol, she thought enviously, to be so young and carefree and *safe*. To have the love of a man like Fraser and the prospect of sharing a home and a family with him here in this secure and untroubled corner of England. Lucky Siriol not to know what it was to carry a burden of guilt that would take a lifetime to pay off. Bethan sighed, knowing it was wrong to envy the girl so much. Since that night ten years ago, a home and a family of her own had never been on the cards for herself, even if Fraser hadn't——

But that was a stupid train of thought. Fraser had shown her long ago how little she meant to him and how amusing he'd found her infatuation. And even though he knew now she had been telling the truth about what she had been doing with her life in the ten years since, there was still an element of hostility in his attitude towards her. He didn't like her, and for all his aunt's championing of her, her presence here was still unwelcome.

For all it was such a warm night, she shivered. It wasn't pleasant to be disliked by someone so intensely, but when it was by the man she loved . . .

She let out a long, despairing sigh. She hadn't wanted to admit it, even to herself, but she couldn't blind herself any longer to the reason why his cruel hostility gave her so much pain. She had loved him years ago as a young girl and she loved him still, only now in her maturity with a depth and power that frightened her. Her mind could tell her it was hopeless, that he was not for her, but her heart and body seemed to have an independent will of their own, leaping to coruscating life whenever he was near.

She only risked laying herself open to more humiliation, for if she stayed here there was always the danger she might betray the way she felt. And anyway, the longer she stayed the more painful it was going to be when the job was over and she must inevitably return to her old life. Lorna, bless her kind, compassionate heart, had no idea of the difficulties she was creating when she had so adamantly opposed Bethan's departure. She was blissfully unaware how much better it would be for all of them if Bethan were allowed to make the break now, before any more damage was done.

But she *did* have an ally against Lorna's well-meaning partisanship—albeit an unlikely one. Fraser himself. He was just as reluctant to have her here as Bethan was to stay. Surely if she spoke to him he would find a way of allowing her to leave without upsetting Lorna too much? The decision made to see him in the morning, she was able to sleep.

CHAPTER FIVE

A WEEK later Bethan was still waiting for the opportunity to speak with Fraser privately. Lorna had determinedly kept her in bed for another two days, cosseting her to the point of acute embarrassment, and although Fraser had looked in politely to see her once or twice, it was only when his aunt was also there, and it wasn't a subject Bethan could bring up in her presence.

The dressings were removed from her hands, and her palms, though still tender, were healing nicely, and at last Dr Stratton had overruled Lorna's caution and given her permission to get up, providing she promised to rest whenever she began to feel in the least tired.

But it began to seem that even though she was up and about, her chances of catching Fraser alone were as remote as they had been while she was still confined to her bed. On her first day, by the time she had come downstairs with both Molly and Lorna fussing round her, Fraser had left the house. He didn't come back for lunch either, and after an afternoon spent stretched out on a lounger in the garden with Lorna she had hung around the sitting-room for quite a while, but there was still no sign of him before Molly came in to set the table for dinner and she was obliged to retreat to her room to wash. He put in a brief appearance as she sat with Lorna sipping their pre-dinner drinks—Bethan opting for apple juice—but he went out again almost immediately and still hadn't returned when she went to bed. And the following days repeated the same pattern, almost as if he was deliberately avoiding her.

When she finally did run him to earth it was so unexpected she could only stand there gaping at him, everything she wanted to say flying out of her head. She had come into the house from the garden to fetch some more silks for Lorna's embroidery, to see him just emerging from his study. He too stood stock-still for a moment, then merely nodding to her, made for the front door.

Seeing her opportunity slipping Bethan said desperately, 'Mr Laurie, could I speak to you, please?'

His dark eyebrows rose, his mouth twisting in bitter mockery. 'You've been calling me Fraser since you were thirteen years old, so what's all this "Mr Laurie"?'

She flushed. 'I'm no longer a child and you're now my employer.'

'My *aunt* is your employer,' he corrected her stiffly. 'And I notice you don't have any difficulty calling her Lorna.'

Bethan's flush deepened. 'I'm sorry if you think I'm too familiar.'

'Oh, for pity's sake!' He turned away as if to put an end to the dispute, then changing his mind turned back again, barking, 'Well? What is it you wanted to speak to me about?'

Bethan hesitated, reluctant to reveal what was on her mind in such a public place as the hall, but the subdued clatter coming from the kitchen reassured her that Molly was busily occupied preparing the lunch and wasn't likely to interrupt them. She lifted her shoulders helplessly. 'All this. The fact that you don't like me and can't stand having me around the place,' she said quietly. 'I did tell your aunt it would be better if I left but she wouldn't hear of it. So I'm asking for your help. I'm sure you could think of a way to let me leave without upsetting her.'

Instead of the curt agreement she had expected, Bethan found her wrist held in an iron grip as she was dragged bodily into his study. Finishing up in a rush half-way across the room she turned to see Fraser leaning against the closed door breathing heavily.

'And what excuse do you suppose she would accept?' he demanded grittily. 'Hugo told her you have no friends in England and nowhere to go from here. So what construction do you think she'll put on your departure? That I've hounded you out, of course. She's already called me to task more than once for my behaviour towards you. Or is that what you want—to leave strife behind you?'

Several days of sitting out in the sun had put some colour back into Bethan's face, but now it all drained away. 'No!' she gasped. 'The last thing I want is to cause any more trouble. I've already told her you were not to blame for my collapse.'

'It was very—generous of you under the circumstances.' The apology seemed to be dragged out of him unwillingly but then he brushed a hand wearily over his face and as he moved away from the door all his earlier anger and antagonism seemed to have left him. 'Bethan, you must see that I can't possibly let you leave yet. Only a few days ago you were too weak to move, and whatever excuses you made to Lorna, I *was* responsible. She'd never forgive me if I turned you out now. And quite frankly,' he added in an undertone, 'I'd never forgive myself.'

Bethan began to tremble inwardly. His former hostility had hurt but it had helped to armour herself against him. Now it was gone she had no defence against the feelings that were overwhelming her, feelings she was afraid she wouldn't be able to go on hiding. 'But there would be nothing to forgive,' she pleaded. 'I'm perfectly fit again now, and I have enough money to keep myself until I can find another job.'

'No!' He turned angrily away from her to the window and she followed him with widened eyes, startled at his vehemence. 'Why bother when you have a perfectly good job here? Or isn't Lorna's obvious affection for you reciprocated?' That biting mockery was back, and Bethan flinched.

'I'm very fond of your aunt. She's been like a mother to me—how I've always dreamed a mother should be.' Immediately she regretted her unguarded reply for Fraser spun round, his eyes narrowed.

'And that's something else! Hugo Fielding gave me chapter and verse of what you've been doing these last ten years, not only your service with the relief agency but your hospital experience before that, your training. So if you were nursing right from the beginning, how did the story that you'd taken off for America to join your mother start?'

Bethan swallowed hard, still reluctant to accuse her stepfather of lying. 'If—if that's what my stepfather wanted everyone to think, it's not so surprising, is it? Not after the way I'd disgraced him?'

'Are you trying to tell me he made it up?' Fraser moved back towards her, all his old antagonism beating against her in waves. 'Oh, no, Bethan, I don't buy that. However much you'd hurt him, he loved you, for God's sake! He'd never have instigated that sickening gossip about you. If he'd wanted to cover up your desertion of him, all he needed to do was tell the truth—that you'd left home to take up nursing.'

'Then I have no explanation to offer.' The lump in her throat made it difficult to speak as she thought of the only father she had ever known, of his generous open-heartedness in giving her as much love as he'd given his own flesh and blood, his only son Mark. That in return she had hurt him she would regret till her dying day, hurt him so much she had killed his love and caused him to turn his back on her. 'Do—do you ever see him?' she asked longingly, still immersed in her own thoughts. Perhaps he might be willing to see her again, if only so she could tell him how sorry she was.

The quality of the sudden silence following her question made her look up to see a thunderstruck expression on Fraser's face. 'I don't know what damage that bomb blast did to you,' he said frowning, 'but you can't have forgotten Charles died nearly six years ago.'

There was a rushing sound in her ears and the room began to swing slowly round her. The next moment she was being thrust into a chair and her head held down between her knees. When at last he allowed her to sit upright again she stared up at him, her green eyes huge with shock in her ashen face. 'Dead!'

Fraser's mouth was tight, his own expression shocked. 'You really didn't know?'

She shook her head. 'How——'

He fought against the utterly lost look in the eyes swimming with tears. 'Oh, come on now. Maybe you *hadn't* heard, but it can't have come as such a shock,' he said harshly. 'Not when you were well aware how desperately ill he was before you did your disappearing act. That's what I find so impossible to understand about you, Bethan. To be a good nurse—and Hugo Fielding assures me you are—you need to have compassion. And yet you showed not an atom of compassion for Charles Latimer.'

His words battered against her but they made no sense when she was still trying to assimilate the fact that her stepfather was dead. The only person in the world who had ever loved her and he was gone. Even though she had spent the last ten years estranged from him the sense of loss was devastating. Now the estrangement really was irrevocable. With his death had gone the last slender hope of his forgiveness.

Slowly Fraser's words began to sink into her consciousness. 'Ill? But he was never ill.'

'Until he had that stroke a few days before your trial, brought on, I might add, by worrying over you. Dear heaven, Bethan!' he exploded fiercely. 'However ashamed of yourself you were, however hard you must have found it to face him, couldn't you have put your own feelings aside and gone to see him when he was asking for you?'

'He had a stroke! But I don't understand . . . why did no one tell me? Oh God . . .' She buried her face in her hands, reeling under this new shock. Why hadn't Mark told her? If it had happened *before* the trial, why hadn't Katy Bourne told her? She must have known. She lifted her head crying hoarsely, 'You *can't* believe I'd have stayed away from him if I'd known!'

But it was obvious that was just what he *did* believe. She sprang to her feet, too anguished to sit still, but her legs were shaky from shock and she had to lean against the desk to steady herself. The consequences of what she had done the night of Ishbel's party were still spreading ten years later, like ripples from a stone dropped into a still pool.

'I didn't know he was ill. I swear I didn't know.' Her voice was raw with emotion and the man watching her took an involuntary step towards her.

'It—it just isn't possible you didn't know.' She was giving the impression that he was crucifying her, and he resented being made to feel guilty. 'You lived in the same house, dammit!'

He was so sure of himself, Bethan thought, so certain he knew all the answers. And he *didn't*. And now there was no reason for her to keep silent. Charles Latimer was dead and the truth couldn't hurt him any more. She straightened up and turned to face her accuser.

'The last time I was in the house in Bancroft Square was when I left it with Mark to drive to Merrifields for Ishbel's party.' Fraser was frowning but she ignored it, going on levelly, 'I was in hospital until they discharged me in time for the magistrate's hearing, and that was the last time I saw my stepfather. I was badly bruised and still in a state of shock. Besides, apparently the house in London had been besieged by reporters. So when Mark suggested sending me down to Cornwall to stay with his old nanny, Katy Bourne, until I was due to appear in the Crown Court, my stepfather thought it

FREE—Lighted Makeup Mirror and Brush Kit. This lighted makeup mirror and brush kit allows plenty of light for those quick touch-ups. It has its own on/off switch and operates on 2 easy-to-replace batteries and bulbs (batteries not included). Holds everything you need for a perfect finished look, yet small enough to slip into your purse or pocket (4-1/8" x 3" closed).

HARLEQUIN READER SERVICE
FREE OFFER CARD

4 FREE BOOKS

A LIGHTED MAKEUP MIRROR AND BRUSH KIT

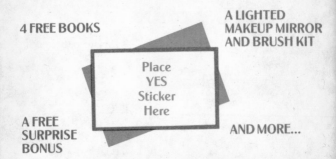

Place
YES
Sticker
Here

A FREE SURPRISE BONUS

AND MORE...

Please send me my four Harlequin Presents novels, free, along with my lighted makeup mirror and brush kit and surprise gift. Then send me eight books every month as they come off the presses and bill me just $1.75 per book (20¢ less than retail), with no extra charges for shipping and handling. If I am not completely satisfied, I may return a shipment and cancel at any time. *The free books and gifts remain mine to keep!*

108 CIP CAKU

Name _____
(PLEASE PRINT)

Address _____ Apt._____

City_____

Prov./State _____ Postal Code/Zip_____

Offer limited to one per household and not valid for present subscribers. Prices subject to change.

PRINTED IN U.S.A.

was a good idea. I spoke to him on the telephone a number of times during the weeks I was with Katy and he sounded ... I had no inkling ...' Her voice faltered but under Fraser's narrowed gaze she pulled herself together.

'I expected him to come and fetch me as the day for the trial drew nearer.' She shivered. 'I—I was very frightened. But a couple of days before, Mark phoned to say I was to make my own way to Colchester by train, telling me he'd booked me into a hotel there to stay overnight, but he never said a word about his father being ill.'

Her green eyes were blank, seeing only the past. 'I still expected to see Charles the next day, but it was Mark who came to collect me from the hotel to accompany me to court. And when it was all over he told me his father had stayed away because I'd disgraced him and he wanted nothing more to do with me.' She ground to a shuddering halt because even at this distance in time she could remember the devastating shock, the sense of being cast adrift like a boat without a rudder.

'*Mark* told you?' Fraser said sharply.

She nodded. 'He said he'd been empowered by his father to settle my fine and to give me a sum of money on condition I never went home or tried to contact him again.'

'And you believed him?' Fraser appeared stunned, though she couldn't think why.

'Of course.' Her throat ached and she shook with self-disgust. 'I'd killed a child in a drunken stupor, caused my stepfather's name to be splashed all over the newspapers. It was no more than I deserved to hear he was disowning me.'

'But that's arrant nonsense!' He looked angry and baffled.

'Is it?' Bethan's mouth twisted bitterly. '*You* obviously thought it was reason enough to cut off all

contact with me. You—and Ishbel——' Her voice
broke on a sob.

'You thought——' He broke off, staring at her
helplessly. 'It was nothing like that. In the first place
Ishbel was never told.'

'Did she have to be told when it was splashed all over
the newspapers? "Diplomat's daughter on manslaughter
charge".' Her voice rose and she had to fight down a
feeling of hysteria. 'At least Katy Bourne wouldn't have
newspapers in the house down in Cornwall.'

'It didn't reach the Australian newspapers.' His
mouth tightened at her puzzlement. 'I pressured Ishbel
into going to Australia with me to stay with relatives.
We flew out the day after her party, before——' He
cleared his throat. 'My father telephoned me with the
news, but I thought it best to keep it from Ishbel.'

'Exactly. Because you no longer thought I was a
suitable friend for her.' All the same, she was glad to
know Ishbel hadn't deliberately severed their friendship.

'No,' he denied harshly. 'Because if I'd told her she
would have insisted on coming straight back to
England with me, which would have brought her back
into Mark Latimer's sphere of influence again when I'd
only just succeeded in getting her away. I left it to you
to tell her as much or as little as you wished when you
wrote to her, but you didn't answer her letters.'

'I never received any,' Bethan said dully, but she
didn't dispute what he'd said.

His explanation made sense. Because she had known
Bethan was in love with her brother, Ishbel at seventeen
had decided *she* was in love with Mark, often telling
Bethan how wonderful it would be if they each married
the other's brother. Bethan had known Fraser
disapproved of his sister seeing so much of Mark, who
had a reputation for wildness and unsavoury friendships, and she'd had doubts herself about her friend
getting involved with him. Whatever Ishbel's feelings—
and somehow Bethan could never believe they ran very

deep—she was quite sure Mark didn't return them, in fact she'd often thought her handsome but often disagreeable stepbrother incapable of loving anyone but himself. So it came as no great surprise to learn that Fraser had gone to the length of whisking his sister off to Australia to split them up.

Fraser sighed. 'I suppose as no one knew where you'd gone, they could hardly have sent Ishbel's letters on.'

'Mark knew,' she said starkly.

His eyes narrowed. 'Mark again.'

Bethan gave a little laugh, though there was no humour in it. 'Actually he was quite kind to me, helping me to find a bedsitter, bringing some of my stuff from home, promising to keep in touch, to let me know if his father relented and was prepared to have me back.' She shivered. 'And all the time keeping back the most important thing—that his father was ill.'

Her green eyes were haunted as she bowed her head. 'And now I have two deaths on my conscience,' she whispered.

Fraser was suddenly grasping her shoulders and shaking her. 'You're not to say that.'

Something in his voice brought her head snapping up and she stared right into his angry grey eyes. 'It's true, though,' she challenged. 'You said yourself it was worry over me that caused my stepfather's stroke and so contributed to his death.'

'But then I didn't know——' His eyes searched her face and his hands tightened on her shoulders as if he was going to draw her to him. The tension that leapt and crackled between them was a tangible thing, stopping Bethan's breath so that her lips parted involuntarily as she swayed towards him, drawn by an irresistible force.

And then as if realising he was still holding her he let her go abruptly, as if the contact burned him. 'If you're telling the truth——' he began.

She drew in a shuddering breath. 'What *reason* could

I have for lying?' she flung at him. That for a few seconds she had come close to revealing her feelings for him had shaken her badly, and yet it hurt and angered her that he should find her touch so repugnant. 'What reason would I have had for refusing to go home after the trial, for refusing to see him, especially if I'd known he was ill and wanting me? It just doesn't make sense. I had everything to lose and nothing to gain by going it alone.'

'I'm not *accusing* you of lying.' He raked both hands through his dark hair. 'In fact the more I hear of this the more convinced I am that you're not.'

Bethan drew in her breath audibly, her heart-beat accelerating. 'You mean you believe me?'

Fraser hesitated, a strange, almost tortured expression on his face. 'Just tell me one thing.' He walked to the fireplace, his thin shirt taut across his broad shoulders as he leaned both hands on the mantelpiece, staring at the unlit logs arranged in the grate, then slowly he turned and faced her. 'Was it true that you let Mark Latimer—that you and he slept together?'

It took a moment before what he was saying sank in. *'No!'* She stared at him with wide, horrified eyes. 'How could you even think it? He was my *brother*.'

'Not by blood,' he said tersely. 'There was no reason——'

'There was every reason,' she contradicted him fiercely, the most cogent being that she had been fathoms deep in love with the man who was now accusing her of what in her own mind would have amounted to incest. She gave a shudder of revulsion. 'He didn't even *like* me, and I certainly never thought of *him* in that way!'

'And if I told you he'd admitted it? Had actually boasted to me that he'd had you more than once?' The skin seemed to be stretched tightly over his cheekbones and his eyes burned into her.

She lifted her chin and met his gaze unwaveringly. 'Then he was lying,' she bit out.

For several seconds longer Fraser held her gaze, then he turned and beat his clenched fist against the mantelpiece. 'Oh God, what a fool I was!' he said thickly. 'What fools we *all* were!'

Bethan watched him in bewilderment, not sure if this outburst meant he believed her or not.

He pushed himself away from the fireplace and looked at her. 'We all forgot Mark Latimer was no great respecter of the truth. And we both forgot how much he hated you.'

She put up her hands as if to ward off what he was saying. 'I know he never liked me, but *hate*?'

'To have done what he did to you? Oh yes.' At her bewildered look he crossed the room quickly and took her hands. 'Don't you see, Bethan? There was no way Charles Latimer could have given Mark those instructions to send you away. For the first few days after his stroke he could barely speak. So if Mark lied to you and to me, he must have lied to his father too. The whole rotten business was one colossal lie! He took advantage of his father's illness to create an unbridgeable rift between you, to get rid of you in effect, telling you one story and his father another, embellishing that one later with lurid details of what you were supposed to be getting up to in America.'

Bethan sank slowly into a chair. 'Oh, no . . .' she breathed, appalled. 'Maybe *I* deserved his hatred, but to do that to his own *father*. And *why* would he do such an awful thing? What did he hope to gain by it?'

'I don't think we have to look far for a reason,' Fraser said sardonically. 'He always regarded you as the cuckoo in the nest, taking *his* share of the cake.'

Bethan raised troubled eyes to his face. 'You mean he was afraid I was taking his father's love away from him? But it just isn't true! Charles loved us both.'

'I don't think it was his father's *affection* he was afraid of sharing,' Fraser retorted tersely. 'Charles Latimer was very comfortably off but he wasn't all *that* wealthy, and we both know Mark would rather spend money than earn it.'

'Money! Oh no, I'm sure you're wrong. Everything Charles had was Mark's; I was only his stepdaughter, after all. And besides, they both knew that having left school I meant to be independent, earn my own living.' But even as she denied it she felt chilled.

And Fraser knew she hadn't even convinced herself. 'As far as Charles was concerned, you were his *daughter* and would be provided for. And Mark was well aware of that, even if you weren't. And he didn't like it one bit. Good lord, I can think of any number of occasions when he deliberately tried to turn his father against you, long before your—accident and Charles's illness gave him the perfect opportunity.' He smiled but there was nothing humorous about it and his voice was grim when he went on. 'And though he might have succeeded all too well in banishing you from the scene, he still didn't get what he wanted. His father still left you half his estate.' He looked down at Bethan's stunned face. 'Doesn't *that* prove Charles still loved you?' His voice was suddenly soft, almost caressing. 'Doesn't it prove he wasn't unforgiving as you seem to believe?'

When there was no response and her expression still remained stunned, he frowned. 'Don't tell me you didn't know about that either! It was advertised for long enough in the newspapers here and in America.'

She shook her head, at last finding her voice. 'You forget, English and American newspapers are not readily available in the African bush.' But Mark could have traced her easily enough if he'd wanted to, she thought dully. He knew which hospital had accepted her for training, and their records would have told him when she had left, a fully fledged SRN, it was to join the relief agency. The knowledge that he had made no attempt to do so weighed like a stone in her heart and finally convinced her of her stepbrother's callous deception.

'Of course, you must have been working for the relief agency by then.' Fraser frowned again, as if the idea angered him. 'I'm sorry if I've given you too many shocks today, but at least *one* good thing has come out of it. You need never go back to such dangerous work again, Bethan. You're a comparatively wealthy young woman.'

How could he *say* that! She shook her head, fighting against the tears of grief that threatened to overcome her. 'I'm not interested in the money. Do you think it means anything to me when all I can think about is that Charles died believing I didn't care about him, believing I'd deserted him just like my mother.' The tears spilled over and she was powerless to stop them.

'Bethan ...' He groaned her name and she felt her hands grasped as he drew her out of the chair and folded her in his arms. 'Please don't cry. You know I never could bear it when you cried.'

Bethan hadn't allowed herself the luxury of tears for years but now the floodgates were open there was no stemming the flow. She sobbed out her grief for the stepfather who had meant so much to her, for the unnecessary pain of his end. She wept for the long years of rejection when she had carried her burden of guilt alone, for the fear and pain she had suffered, and there were tears of contrition too, for the irresponsible act that had begun the mess she had made of her life on the night of Ishbel's party.

And under all this storm of emotion, not consciously recognised but there all the same, was the feeling of rightness that it was Fraser's strong body that was supporting her, his arms that circled her offering comfort, just as he had so many times during the smaller griefs of her adolescence. Even when the storm began to subside she felt no self-consciousness at first.

'Bethan, it does no good to break your heart over it now.' Fraser's voice was strained, and as she raised her head, one hand came up to wipe her tears away with his

fingers, an expression almost of tenderness on his face.
'Just remember Charles loved you right up to the end,
and you loved him. None of Mark's manipulating
changed that.'

A measure of peace settled over Bethan's heart,
promoted partly from the release of years of bottled-up
emotion and partly from Fraser's words.

'Thank you.' She smiled up at him, her soft mouth
tremulous, the lashes fringing her luminous green eyes
spiky from the tears she had shed, and because she wore
no make-up, no mascara to make clown-like runnels, it
gave her face an innocently childlike beauty that caught
at the heart-strings of the man holding her, bringing the
barriers he had erected against her, which had been
severely tested during the last hour, finally crashing
down.

But Bethan, aware only of a subtle change in the way
he was holding her, responded to it mindlessly, letting
her head fall back against his chest, her own arms
stealing round his waist, her hands spread against his
muscled back moving with an unknowing sensuality.
Rational thought was suspended as her body surren-
dered to the longing to hold him with a sense of
homecoming, that this was where she belonged. When
his arms tightened round her, when the hard thrust of
his body left her in no doubt of his arousal, she felt only
a wild elation.

It was his audible gasp and his agonised, 'Bethan!'
as her mouth sought the tanned column of his throat
that brought the alarm-bells clamouring in her head.
Just so had he appeared to want her once before, that
evening in the summer-house at Merrifields when she
had all but offered herself to him. Then, as now, she
had dreamed of an untold happiness but had found
only rejection and humiliation. The sense of belonging
in his arms was an illusion. She had never belonged
there for he had never loved her. He belonged to
Siriol now, the girl he was engaged to marry, and

Bethan could feel only shame at having forgotten that even momentarily.

She stiffened, pushing away from him. 'I'm sorry, I didn't mean to embarrass you.' She endeavoured to keep her voice light.

His mouth quirked upwards and his eyes smiled while his arms seemed reluctant to let her go. 'Do I look embarrassed?'

She flushed and stepped away from him firmly. 'No, but *I* am.' Desperately she cast around for something acceptable to say that would explain her mindless response to him without exposing her true feelings, and rushed on, 'I wouldn't want you to think I was still suffering from that childish infatuation I inflicted on you years ago. You'll have to put that little show of feminine weakness down to all the shocks I've received this morning.'

She watched the smile die out of his eyes. 'Bethan, I don't know what——'

But she didn't want to listen to what *his* excuse might be, and broke in quickly with a laugh that even in her own ears sounded hollow. 'You will thank Siriol, won't you, for loaning me your shoulder to cry on?'

His face was suddenly blank and remote, and into the crashing silence Lorna's voice called across the hall, 'Bethan, where are you? My dear, are you all right?'

Bethan seized her opportunity to escape, dragging open the study door.

'Oh there you are. You were gone so long I thought you might be feeling ill.' Lorna sounded relieved but looked at her curiously.

'No, I'm fine. I—Fraser and I—I mean, I bumped into him when I came into the house and as I wanted to speak to him——'

She faltered to a stop as Fraser's voice behind her said, 'That's right, Lorna. Bethan had some silly idea that I'd be happier if she left Vine House. It's all right,' he calmed his aunt who had begun to protest. 'I think

I've convinced her she was wrong and she's agreed to stay. Isn't that right, Bethan?' His tone was polite, even friendly, but his eyes were steely, challenging her to deny his assertion.

And Bethan knew she couldn't meet that challenge when Lorna was looking so pleased. 'That's right,' she agreed reluctantly, and wondered how she was going to survive the next few weeks.

CHAPTER SIX

IMMEDIATELY on leaving the study, Fraser drove away in his sleek Mercedes sports car and didn't return to lunch, much to Bethan's relief. But even without his presence she found Lorna's eager conversation a strain, especially when the older woman several times declared how delighted she was Bethan and Fraser had become friends. She had to make an enormous effort to respond when her mind was seething with so many other things.

It wasn't until she had pulled the sun-loungers into the shade of a huge white lilac-tree and settled Lorna down for her afternoon rest that she had the opportunity to think about what she had learned from Fraser that morning.

The shock of learning her stepfather was dead had numbed her to the enormity of what Mark had done, and even now she found it hard to credit he could be so monstrously selfish, not only indifferent to her own feelings, but to the extra suffering he had inflicted on his father at a time when Charles had been virtually helpless.

She had always known Mark resented her, even before his father had married her mother and installed them in his home. A sulky fifteen to her own shy and awkward ten, he had made no attempt to welcome her into his family or even to be friendly. Indeed, while their parents had been away on their honeymoon, leaving Bethan and Mark in the care of the housekeeper at the house in Bancroft Square, he had gone out of his way to make her feel an unwanted outsider, mocking her in front of his friends, only hiding his hostility in front of the staff, and once, when caught out by the housekeeper in one of his calculated humiliations he

107

had spitefully twisted her arm behind her back until she had fallen on her knees in agony to punish her for the reprimand he had received.

And Bethan had been helpless in the face of his enmity. When their parents had returned home he had been careful to treat her with simulated friendliness in their presence, giving them an entirely false impression that he welcomed a younger sister. Only when his father had announced his intention of legally adopting Bethan had he betrayed his true feelings with a fit of temper, and that he had soon apologised for, to outsiders apparently accepting Bethan's place in his father's affections. But Bethan had never been left in any doubt of his continuing resentment, especially when his father was sent abroad on another assignment and her mother had refused to go with him, preferring to stay in London where her friendships with other men began to cause talk.

She had never been close to her beautiful but shallow mother, and had often wondered what had prompted her to motherhood in the first place when it interested her so little and she was so unsuited to it. Bethan had no recollection of her father as he had died before she was two years old, and she had been brought up by a series of housekeepers while a succession of 'uncles' touched the periphery of her young life.

When Bethan had first been introduced to Charles Latimer she had liked him instantly because he was the first of her mother's men friends ever to take an interest in her, and when her mother had announced they were to marry, she had been beside herself with delight.

Remembering how she had expected they would all live happily ever after, Bethan sighed. She would never understand what had constantly driven her mother to seek male adulation, never understand how she could have thrown aside a good marriage and the love of a man like Charles Latimer in search for new conquests and excitement. And while she could never condone her mother's behaviour either, she had sometimes wondered if Mark's dislike of his father's remarriage had contributed to its break-up. Certainly when the scandal broke and her mother ran off to America with her film-star lover, Mark had been triumphant, though his triumph had been short-lived when it became clear the mother's sins were not to be visited on Bethan and that Charles Latimer had no intention of relinquishing his adopted daughter.

Mark's fury had been frightening, but he had been eighteen by then and away at university, and Bethan herself was sent to boarding-school, so most of the time she was free of his resentment and spite. And when they did have to spend time together during the holidays, Fraser Laurie had often been around to protect her from the worst of Mark's malice. It was true, though, what Fraser had said this morning; Mark had lost no opportunity to manipulate her into situations that would make his father think badly of her. Even so, she'd had no idea he hated her so much he was prepared to go to such lengths to be rid of her. She made no excuses for her own culpability in sparking off the disaster, but that Mark could have had so little feeling for his father sickened her.

She let her mind go back to that terrible time between the magistrate's hearing and her trial at the Crown Court, trying to remember the details, and realised the clues *had* been there if only she hadn't been so blinded by her own shock and enormous guilt to see them. It was the guilt that had led her to accept without question Mark's shattering news that her stepfather had done with her. And yet would Charles have telephoned her so regularly at Katy Bourne's cottage in Cornwall if he had been thinking of disowning her? He had been disappointed in her, saddened by the trouble she was in and deeply anxious, but he had never once appeared unforgiving. The loving concern had still been there in his voice, in his insistence that she mustn't let herself

brood over what had happened. Shouldn't she have
wondered that it was *Mark* who had telephoned with
the instructions that she was to make her own way to
Colchester for the trial, staying overnight there in a
hotel instead of breaking her journey in London to stay
at the house? Katy had taken the call and had seemed
upset when she had called Bethan to the phone, but too
wrapped up in her own problems, Bethan had thought
nothing of it at the time. Perhaps Mark had broken the
news of his father's illness to Katy then, but had asked
her not to mention it. If he had already decided to take
advantage of the situation, it would have been
reasonable to suggest he didn't want Bethan worried
before her trial, and he could be fairly certain she
wouldn't hear of it from any other source as the cottage
was so isolated and Katy, eccentric in her retirement,
wouldn't have television or newspapers in the house
and rarely listened to the radio.

She should have suspected Mark's kindness during
and after her trial too, since it was so uncharacteristic.
But again, weighed down by guilt, especially as the
mother of the child she had killed had screamed at her
outside the courthouse after her release, shocked by her
stepfather's rejection and the fact that as none of her
friends had been in touch they must regard her as
beyond the pale too, she had been too grateful for
Mark's sudden sympathy to question it.

And all the time Charles Latimer had been lying
there in hospital fighting for his life, asking for her,
worrying probably when she didn't come. Tears
squeezed between her closed eyelids for the pity of it all,
for the hurt her apparent desertion had inflicted on
him.

The air was warm in that sheltered spot, the breeze
stirring the lilac-tree into a soothing rustle. Worn out
by emotion, Bethan slept.

The sudden coolness as a tall figure blocked out the
sun jerked her awake and she opened her eyes to see

Fraser standing over her. 'Isn't collapsing from exhaustion enough for you? Do you want sunstroke as well?' he demanded harshly, and it was only then Bethan realised the patch of shade had moved, and she had been sleeping in the full sun.

She struggled groggily to her feet and went to move the lounger, but Fraser beat her to it, the sound of it dragging over the flagstones waking Lorna.

'Oh, Fraser, you've brought the tea out I see. Thank you, my dear. Are you going to join us?'

To Bethan's consternation he readily agreed, and by the time she had poured out and handed him his cup he was sitting on the lounger she had just vacated. 'Don't hover like a moth, sit down.' He patted the cushion beside him.

'I can fetch another chair,' she said quickly, but he grasped her wrist.

'It's hardly worth the effort when you can share with me,' he said lazily, but there was nothing lazy about his increased pressure on her wrist and she reluctantly obeyed, flushing when he added in an undertone, 'You wouldn't want Lorna to think we *hadn't* settled our differences, would you?'

He stayed for half an hour and although Lorna did most of the talking, Bethan was acutely aware of his brooding presence.

He was at home for dinner that evening too, and there was no Siriol to take his attention, and after they had drunk their coffee in the sitting-room he showed no signs of going out or even retiring to his study. This time the suggestion that Bethan should pit her wits against him at chess came from Fraser himself and not his aunt. She would have liked to refuse but could think of no excuse, especially as Lorna was eager to witness the match, so she had no alternative but to fetch out the board.

At first she was too tensely aware of his nearness across the small table, of the strength of his lean,

tanned hands with their sprinkling of dark hairs to
concentrate on the game, but after two foolish moves
and his mocking reaction to them put her on her mettle,
she found she was actually beginning to enjoy pitting
her wits against his, pleased at his surprise when she
blocked one of his gambits and at the knowledge that
he wasn't having the walkover he expected.

That he was enjoying the battle too was apparent
from the frown of irritation on his face when the door
opened and Siriol came in with a rush. 'Darling, I
thought you were coming over this evening,' she said
reproachfully, kissing his cheek as she perched on the
arm of his chair.

'I don't remember making any such promise,' Fraser
said coolly.

'I—I know you didn't, darling, but I usually see you
some time in the evening.' Such an unenthusiastic
reception had obviously shaken her.

'I fancied a game of chess tonight and as neither you
nor your father play . . .' Fraser made no attempt to
placate his fiancée, indeed still seemed to be irritated by
the interruption.

Bethan might envy Siriol but she couldn't help liking
her, and seeing the uncertainty in the younger girl's
dark eyes, feeling sorry for her too. 'But now you're
here I know he'll find your company much more
stimulating than mine.' She smiled at Siriol reassuringly.
'I don't mind packing this up.'

'A tactical retreat? Afraid I'm going to wipe the floor
with you?' Fraser's voice was light but the tightening
of his jaw told Bethan he wasn't pleased at her
abandonment of the game, and Siriol must have
realised that too because she said at once, 'Oh, please
don't let me interrupt. I can talk to Lorna till you're
finished.'

As if to prevent any more argument she went to sit
on a padded stool at Lorna's feet. Fraser directed a
sardonic glance at Bethan, who glared back at him.

Heavens, but he was arrogant! That was his fiancée he'd just snubbed, the woman he was going to marry! And only this morning——

Bethan's face flooded with colour. It was bad enough to remember those moments this morning when she had been anything but reluctant in Fraser's arms, but to remember it in the presence of his fiancée made her behaviour seem all the more unforgivable. Filled with guilty embarrassment she was too conscious of Siriol's light voice chattering to Lorna to concentrate on the chessboard and made a stupid move. Instantly aware of Fraser's sardonic gaze fixed on her flushed cheeks as if he was reading her guilty thoughts, her hands trembled. From then on she didn't even try, throwing the game away because she only wanted it to be finished.

Fraser made no comment until his aunt asked what he thought of Bethan's game. 'Disappointing,' he said forthrightly. 'Oh, she was very promising to start with, but then she collapsed like a house of cards.' He reached down and pulled Siriol to her feet. 'Perhaps she was feeling guilty at keeping me from you, darling.'

Bethan resented being talked about as if she wasn't there and disliked the accuracy with which he had guessed her motives, but she managed to hide her feelings, saying quietly, 'I think I'm just tired. If you're ready for bed now, Lorna . . .'

But tired as she was, Bethan found sleep elusive. She kept seeing again Fraser's brooding eyes on her as she had helped his aunt from the room, leaving him and Siriol alone together. And she couldn't seem to stop herself imagining the two of them after she and Lorna had gone. Had Fraser apologised to Siriol for his lack of welcome? And had Siriol readily forgiven him in his arms? She found herself remembering herself in those same arms and had to roll herself into a ball to suppress the deep ache of longing inside her.

After her restless night she woke very early, her bedside clock telling her it was only six o'clock, but

knowing she would not get back to sleep she rose and
dressed, and moving quietly so as not to disturb anyone
else she slipped downstairs and let herself out into the
garden. The early-morning air was chill and damp, a
thick mist hanging over the vineyard beyond the wall
but the sun shining with a pearly light through it
promised a hot day later on. A rambler-rose climbed up
the wall in a sheltered corner, its scent elusive as it
waited for the heat of the sun to draw it out. Bethan
moved towards it breathing deeply.

A sound broke the stillness and turning towards it
she saw Fraser emerge from the summer-house between
the two walled gardens. He wore only minuscule
bathing trunks and his tanned skin glistened with water.
He was rubbing his hair with a towel as he walked back
towards the house, obviously having been for a swim in
the pool, and Bethan couldn't drag her eyes away,
drinking in every attractive line of his body as if to store
it in her memory; the wide, powerful shoulders, the
dark hair roughening his chest and veeing down to his
flat, taut stomach while long, muscled legs moved
lithely from narrow hips.

It was some moments before she realised he had
removed the towel from his head and was watching her
watching him, and even at a distance she could see the
hard mockery in his face. She nodded an embarrassed
'Good morning,' and turned away again, pretending an
interest in the rose and wishing there were somewhere
she could hide herself.

He didn't return her greeting and she thought he had
carried on to the house so she nearly jumped out of her
skin when his voice right behind her said, 'It's a very
common variety, you know, and hardly warrants such
close scrutiny.'

She turned to find him standing so close she could
feel his body heat, smell the tang of chlorine still
adhering to his skin, and for a moment she was almost
overcome by the urge to reach out and touch him.

Moistening her suddenly dry lips she said as coolly as her hammering heart would allow, 'Even a common dandelion would warrant attention in some of the places I've been.'

His mouth compressed and his dark brows drew together as if her remark had angered him, but all he said was, 'You're an early bird. Lorna won't be up for a couple of hours yet.'

'I'm used to getting up early. It's often been the only really comfortable time to work.' Not that it was particularly comfortable right now. The clammy dampness penetrated her thin blouse yet Fraser, disconcertingly naked except for his bathing trunks, appeared not to feel it at all. She tried, not quite successfully, to repress a shiver.

'Cold?' His eagle eye missed nothing.

'Just a little,' she admitted. 'I suppose I'm not fully acclimatised yet.' But it wasn't just the dampness that was making her shiver. She found Fraser's closeness very disturbing and wished he would move away. 'You'll catch cold if you stand around here for long,' she suggested, but he only grinned.

'I never catch cold,' he claimed, and Bethan believed him. 'Anyway it's going to be a scorcher when this mist clears.'

'Yes, I thought it might. Perhaps it'll be hot enough for Lorna to go in the pool. She told me how keen she is to swim when the weather's suitable.'

Fraser frowned. 'I don't think that's such a good idea. I don't like her going in the pool unless I'm there. She finds it rather difficult to get out.'

'But I'll be there to help her.' Bethan's hackles rose at the implication that he didn't believe her capable.

'And if *you* get into difficulties? Only a week ago you were too weak to get out of bed. No, for the safety of *both* of you, you won't go in unless I'm there,' he said arrogantly. 'I'll try to spare a few minutes after you've both had your rest this afternoon.'

And having dictated his terms he turned and made his leisurely way back to the house, leaving Bethan fuming.

The weather did turn hot, a real scorching June day without a puff of breeze, and after most of the morning spent in the garden, Lorna elected to take her after-lunch rest in the cool of the sitting-room. Bethan found she couldn't settle and the more she thought about it, the more appealing the idea of a swim to cool off became. Fraser hadn't actually said *she* wasn't to go in alone. It had been his aunt's safety he'd been concerned about. Anyway he need never know. And if she had already had her swim, she could cry off later if he *did* come back. The thought carried her upstairs to rummage through her drawer for her swimsuit, and while she didn't consciously admit the thought of displaying her scarred back in front of Fraser bothered her, it was there in her subconscious.

Bethan eyed her reflection in the mirror wryly. She was still too thin, though the delicious cooking Molly had been tempting her with the last few weeks had given her back a little of her feminine curves, but the black, one-piece bathing-suit did little to flatter her, being juvenile in the extreme. She shrugged, slipping a cotton shirt over it, then collecting a towel from the bathroom she left the house quietly and made for the pool.

The water sparkled invitingly in the sunlight and the sense of privacy was reassuring. Throwing off the cotton shirt and dropping it with the towel on one of the loungers, she stood on the edge of the pool for a moment, enjoying the sun on her skin, then with unconscious grace, dived in.

There had been so little opportunity in recent years to indulge in a sport she had loved as a young girl, when in some of the places she had worked enough water to wash in had been a luxury, and she swam with lazy, unhurried strokes, revelling in the silky coolness against her heated skin. But in spite of the pleasant buoyancy of the water she found she soon tired and rolled over to float on her back, gazing up at the arching sky with only the occasional cotton-wool puff of cloud to break the clear blue. Doves cooed somewhere out of sight and the house-martins that nested in the eaves of the summer-house swooped twittering after unsuspecting insects. The sheer peacefulness was like a healing balm and Bethan felt more relaxed than she could ever remember.

And then the peace was splintered into fragments by a harsh voice demanding, 'What the *hell* are you doing? Come out of there, Bethan. This minute.'

Her body jerked with guilty apprehension and she went under, coming up coughing and spluttering to see Fraser poised on the edge of the pool as if for two pins he'd jump in fully clothed and drag her out, every line of his stance betraying his fury.

Feeling suddenly cold despite the heat of the sun on her shoulders, Bethan made for the steps, missing her footing and banging her shin in her haste to climb them before he reached her.

'Don't you listen?' He looked as if he was about to grab her and shake her and she stepped back apprehensively. 'Didn't you hear me tell you not to go into the pool unless I was here?'

'You told me not to take *Lorna* into the pool unless you were here,' she retorted defensively. 'You didn't say anything about *me* not going in alone.'

'I would have thought your own common sense would have told you,' he said witheringly. 'If you'd collapsed again ...' He took a deep breath and his voice was not quite steady. 'It doesn't bear thinking about.'

Bethan gazed up at him, her eyes wide and questioning. Did he *care* about what happened to her? It was a heady thought but she dismissed it at once. Of course he didn't, at least no more than he would care about the welfare of anyone staying under his roof. She could just imagine the figure she must cut, her skinniness revealed by her unflattering bathing-suit, unattractive, no longer even young, and now disfigured too. It was then she realised in a moment of illogical panic that Fraser was standing between her and her shirt and towel still lying on the lounger.

'I'm sorry. I suppose it was very thoughtless of me.' She bowed her head, trying to think how she could edge round him to reach her towel without turning her back on him, little realising her hair, still dripping and plastered to her head, had parted along the lines of her scalp wounds.

She heard his harshly indrawn breath even as she felt his hands touch her head. 'Oh God! And you worked *four hours* in the vineyard with injuries like these! In the name of heaven, Bethan, why didn't you *tell* me?'

But she couldn't answer him because his hands had fallen to her shoulders and then slid round her back as he pulled her against him. She just had time to remember how often he had held her protectively like this in the past, comforting her when she'd been hurt, and then she felt his caressing hands still, his body stiffen, and knew he had felt the puckered skin of her disfigured back.

She tried to pull away, but although his hands were gentle there was no escaping their hold as slowly he turned her round. His face was grey beneath his tan, his eyes appalled when he finally turned her back to face him again.

'Is this why you swam alone, because you didn't want anyone to see?' His harshly spoken question confirmed what she already knew, that he found her scars repulsive. It brought her chin up defensively and bright flags of colour to her cheeks.

'Why not? It's hardly a sight I would wish to inflict on anyone. Now, if you'd let me get my towel . . .'

Something flashed in his grey eyes that might have been anger or might have been something else she couldn't define before he released her, and she could feel those eyes burning into her scarred back as she walked away from him. Only he hadn't stayed by the pool. As she reached for her towel he took it from her, draping it gently round her.

'You don't have to feel self-conscious about it here, Bethan,' he said quietly, and she bent her head, suddenly feeling ashamed of her oversensitivity.

'No. It's stupid to mind if people find me repulsive when I know I was the lucky one. At least I'm still alive. The friend I was with was killed.'

She saw his hands clench. 'Don't talk ridiculous! Your scars make me feel—angry for what you've been through, guilty even, to have had things so easy when you—but repulsive . . . oh no. Anything but!'

His vehemence surprised her into looking up at him to catch a strange, almost fiercely possessive look on his face. His next question was equally surprising. 'Your friend who was killed, it was a man friend?'

He seemed oddly intent on peopling her last few years with men, Bethan thought. It wasn't the first time he had brought the subject up, but before he'd been blunt enough to refer to them as lovers. She found it ludicrous that he should believe her to be irresistible to other men when he had found her totally resistible himself. And in this instance she found his question in bad taste.

'Betty-Lou was a nurse,' she said quietly, and had the satisfaction of seeing a faint redness creep over his cheekbones. 'American. We were on our way to her fiancé's apartment—Mike was a doctor on the team— for a farewell party when the shell-blast hit us. They were both leaving Lebanon the following day, going back to America to get married. Only there was no wedding, only Betty-Lou's funeral.' A tear trickled down her cheek at the appalling snuffing out of such a life.

As if he couldn't help himself, Fraser reached out and squeezed her shoulders lightly. 'I'm sorry. Life does hand out some dirty deals sometimes.'

She knew he was attempting to offer comfort but could find none. 'Helped along by the human race. Man's inhumanity to man. I've seen enough of that these last few years.' There was bitter disillusion in her voice, in the twist of her soft mouth. 'And it was particularly unfair that Betty-Lou had to be the one to die when she had so much to live for.'

'You make it sound as if you wish *you'd* been the one to die,' he accused harshly. 'You can't mean that.'

'Why not?' She lifted haunted eyes to his face. 'There would have been a certain poetic justice about it.'

His expression repudiated what she was saying. 'But you're still young. *You've* got so much to live for too, especially now you don't have to go on working for the relief agency. The money your stepfather left you,' he reminded her when she looked at him blankly.

'What difference does that make to me working for the agency?' she demanded.

'All the difference in the world, I should think.' He shook her in an oddly gentle exasperation. 'Bethan, don't you *want* to make a life of your own? A home, husband, family?'

A spasm of intense pain flickered across her face. There was only one man she had ever wanted to share her life with and that was the man raking so carelessly at her feelings now. A man who had never wanted to share that dream, who had shown her in the cruellest way possible that he had no time for her.

She was back in the twilit garden at Merrifields, running across the lawn with wings on her heels because although Fraser had brought Lisa Farraday along to the party, Ishbel had just told her he wanted to see her—Bethan—in the summer-house. It was more of a folly really, surrounded by rampant rhododendrons, the stonework beginning to crumble, and it was empty when she reached it so she sat down on the padded cushion of the wide stone seat to wait. She waited a long time—or it seemed very long in her impatience—and she was beginning to wonder if Ishbel had been playing a joke when she heard footsteps. She couldn't see clearly in the half-light as he stepped through the open doorway but her senses recognised him at once, springing tinglingly alive.

'Fraser . . .' She stood up and moved towards him. He had kissed her only a few days ago and she desperately wanted him to kiss her again. And he must want to, mustn't he, if he had asked her to meet him here in this secluded spot far away from the high jinks of Ishbel's party. The knowledge gave her confidence and she wound her arms round his neck, pulling his mouth down to her own. The initiative was only hers for a few seconds and then he was growling low in his throat, his arms tightening crushingly round her as he deepened the kiss, parting her lips, plundering her moist sweetness until her head swam and a deep ache started in the pit of her stomach, making her legs weak.

His mouth left hers to trace a trail of fire across her cheek to her ear as his fingers twined in her long, fiery hair to draw her head back and leave the column of her throat exposed to his questing mouth. The bootlace strap of her dress slipped and she heard the raggedness of his breathing as his head plunged lower, his mouth exploring the naked globe of her breast, his tongue and teeth teasing the rosebud peak until she gasped with pleasure, her body arching against him in involuntary female entreaty.

Never had a man touched her so intimately before, but she felt no shame, not even shyness, and although the sensations he was arousing in her were entirely new, they were entirely natural, as if her body had been made for this man's lovemaking alone. She had loved him for so long, her first, her only love, a love that had once been content just to know he existed, content with a

smile, a few teasing words, a friendly touch. But now it
was a love that demanded so much more, a woman's
love for a man. The first time he had kissed her he had
lit a fire that wouldn't be quenched, even when he
inexplicably reverted to treating her like a child again.

Now he had both firm young breasts free of their
constricting covering of pale green chiffon and the
touch of his strong hands, the expression on his face as
he looked at her nakedness brought the blood surging
hotly through her viens. He wasn't seeing her as a child
now, but as a woman. And he wouldn't have left the
party, wouldn't have asked her to meet him here if he
didn't love her too. She pulled his head down to her
breasts with a fierce joy.

He groaned, burying his face against the smooth, silky
swell, then gathering her up he carried her to the wide
padded seat, his weight crushing her as he lay against
her, leaving her in no doubt as to his desire for her. Her
hands slid inside his shirt, exploring the hair-roughened
chest, the taut muscles of his shoulders and back,
seeming to know instinctively how to please him. And
please him she did, for he shuddered against her, his
own caresses becoming more urgent, more demanding.

Lost to everything but the incandescent flame he lit
inside her, the overwhelming need to be one with him,
to know the fulfilment of their love, she moved against
him, begging, 'Love me, Fraser. Oh, darling, please love
me . . .'

Bethan hugged the towel even closer round her, the
memory of how abjectly she had begged for his love as
searingly humiliating now as it had been then. For he
had refused her. One moment he had seemed to be on
fire for her and the next he had thrust himself away
from her, his appalled, 'Oh, God, I must be mad!' like
the stab of a stiletto in her heart.

'Is this why you got me out here to the summer-
house, to offer yourself to me?' He stood over her, his
voice accusing, and she could only stare up at him in

hurt bewilderment, too stunned to remind him he had asked *her* to meet him here, and what to Bethan had seemed so right, so natural, so—inevitable, was suddenly cheap and sordid because she had been mistaken. Fraser *didn't* love her. Oh, he had wanted her momentarily, perhaps as any man might be tempted by what she had offered, but he didn't feel about her the way she felt about him, and the knowledge brought an involuntary gasp of anguish.

'Beth, you're very young——' His voice was suddenly more gentle but he couldn't know his reference to her youth only added salt to the wound he had inflicted, and anyway at that moment Lisa Farraday's imperative tones calling 'Fraser? Fraser, where are you?' not far away had his head jerking up, whatever he had been going to say forgotten.

'For God's sake cover yourself up, Beth,' he said harshly, and strode to the door.

And as Bethan scrabbled at the straps of her dress to cover her breasts she heard Lisa Farraday say, 'Darling, I thought you'd need rescuing by now.'

She didn't catch the words of Fraser's low-voiced reply but she heard their shared laughter, and every inch of her skin burned with humiliation while something seemed to die inside her.

Perhaps it wasn't so surprising that she had gone off the rails that night and got drunk. Not that it excused the appalling thing she had done. It was a pity that scene in the summer-house with Fraser couldn't have been wiped off her memory as the rest of that awful night had been, but her own wanton behaviour and Fraser's rejection of it had been branded on her consciousness so deeply it had been the only thing she *had* remembered the following day when she had woken up in hospital to find a policeman sitting by her bedside.

And now the man who had so callously smashed her girlish dreams was asking if she had never thought of settling down with a husband and family. What would he say, she wondered, if she told him that he was the only husband she had ever wanted, *his* children the only children she wanted to bear? He would be terribly embarrassed, of course, and she would never dream of telling him. What had been out of her reach ten years ago was even more unattainable now.

She shrugged with pretended indifference. 'Plain girls like me have to set their sights on other aims,' she said flatly, the touch of bitterness more revealing than she knew when she added, 'I learned that at a very early age.'

CHAPTER SEVEN

'FISHING for compliments, Bethan?' Fraser derided, yet his eyes narrowed because she sounded as if she really believed that. 'You were never plain in your life! Good Lord, you must see that every time you look in your mirror.' His voice roughened. 'Don't tell me there haven't been men in plenty to tell you so.'

Her wide green eyes searched his face for signs of the mockery she knew must be there. She could find none but still shook her head in flat rejection of his assertion. Oh, some of her male colleagues had made tentative advances during the last ten years, but then they had shared some pretty lonely assignments and when the choice of female companionship was so limited she had never been foolish enough to read anything into it beyond simple friendship. And friendship was all she had been able to accept from them. Only one man had ever had the power to stir her, and he hadn't found her attractive enough to return her feelings.

And why should he? she asked herself. If her own mother hadn't been able to love her, why should she have expected it of Fraser? Only Charles Latimer had ever found anything in her to love, and in spite of all the suffering she had caused him, his love still stretched out beyond the grave. But if Fraser believed Charles's love—in the form of his legacy—would free her from the burden of guilt she carried, he couldn't be more wrong.

'You're very flattering, but my attractions, real *or* imaginary, are neither here nor there.' She lifted her chin, looking at him levelly, and the hint of steel beneath her extreme fragility had never been more apparent. 'The fact is, my life is no longer my own. I forfeited the right to pursue my own happiness when I killed that child.'

She saw the shock in his face, watched it with a kind of curious detachment. 'But, Bethan, that was ten years ago!' he protested. 'You can't *still* be punishing yourself for a few moments' irresponsibility that happened when you were little more than a child yourself.'

She wondered at his shocked dismay, considering his own silent condemnation of her at the time and his open contempt for her since he had discovered her living in his aunt's home. But his condemnation couldn't be any greater than her condemnation of herself. 'A few moments was all it took, and that little girl is *still* dead,' she said flatly. 'You surely don't think that's something I could just walk away from ... forget?'

Fraser made a forceful, negating gesture with his hand, but she could see from the expression on his face that was what he *had* thought. 'Forget? Well, perhaps not, but surely after all this time you could begin to forgive yourself?' He sounded angry and she couldn't imagine why. What could it possibly matter to him?

She shook her head. 'You make it sound so easy, but how can you possibly know what it's like to be responsible for the death of another human being?' She turned away from him, still huddled in the towel, to stare unseeingly across the drowsing garden. 'Oh, there have been times when I've almost been able to forget,' she said softly, thinking aloud, 'when I've been too bone-weary to think of anything but the next job to be done. Times of personal danger, times of sheer bloody frustration when I've had to watch babies suffering from exhaustion and malnutrition die because they've given up, too apathetic to put up a fight. But since I've been back in England she's often been on my mind, the little girl I killed.' Her throat ached with regret. 'Perhaps because for the first time since it happened I've had *time* to think. She would have been eighteen now, a young woman, perhaps falling in love, looking forward to being married, having a family of her own . . .' Her voice broke on a choked sob. 'So how can I ever forgive myself? And how can I ever expect to enjoy the things I deprived her of?'

His hands on her shoulders were unexpectedly gentle as he turned her round to face him. 'Bethan . . .'

She looked up at him with huge, haunted eyes. For just a few minutes she had forgotten his presence and felt shocked and bewildered at how much of herself she had revealed, unable to forget that the last time she had exposed her deepest feelings to him, he had turned away from her, laughed at her.

'I'm sorry.' She lowered her head as embarrassed colour stained her cheeks. 'I don't know what got into me. I've never spoken about it to anyone before. Ironic that I should unburden myself now, to you of all people.'

His hands tightened their grip convulsively as he pulled her against him. 'Why do you say that? Me of all people?' There was a note in his voice that she might have believed was pain if she hadn't known she had no power to hurt him. 'There was a time, Bethan, when I was the first person you would have confided in.'

But that had been a long time ago, before she had discovered he was sharing the joke of her unrequited love for him with his current girlfriend. She stiffened and tried to pull away from his hold as she said, 'Yes, you were very patient, but I'm no longer an importunate child, and I have no excuse for inflicting my cares on someone who could have no possible interest in them.'

'How can you *say* that?' He refused to let her go, shaking her with a restrained violence.

Only when an uncertain voice said, 'Fraser . . .?' did his hands fall to his sides as his indrawn breath hissed in exasperation. Following the direction of his eyes,

Bethan was dismayed to see Siriol standing watching them from the shadow of the summer-house, her face stricken.

She had no idea how long the other girl had been there but there was no mistaking the fact that Siriol was putting an entirely wrong construction on the apparently intimate scene she had witnessed. Leaping in to retrieve the situation Bethan forced a smile to her face as she moved away from Fraser. 'I'm afraid your fiancé's cross with me. He's been ticking me off for swimming alone in the pool.' It wasn't entirely a lie because that was how this confrontation with Fraser had begun, and if it had been downright untruth it would have been worth it to see Siriol's uncertainty evaporate, her pretty face lighten. 'And now if you'll excuse me,' she went on, 'it's time I went to see if Lorna's woken yet.'

She made her escape, but it wasn't his fiancée Fraser's eyes followed or whose conversation engaged his attention. Agreeing absently to her suggestion that they should swim, he brooded on his recent conversation with Bethan. And to think only a few days ago he had been telling himself she'd got off lightly! Lightly! Dear God, only now was he beginning to understand what she'd gone through, what she was still suffering.

Knowing herself responsible for someone's death would have been hard enough for any eighteen-year-old girl to come to terms with, even with the help and support of her family and friends, but thanks to her stepbrother's machinations Bethan had had no support at all. She'd had to face up to her guilt and remorse entirely alone, believing what she had done to be so unforgivable that the family and friends she had grown up with wanted nothing more to do with her. Little wonder that her sense of guilt was so deep-rooted she hadn't been able to put the tragic episode behind her. And he had to bear some of the responsibility for that himself. He'd stood aside and let it happen, believing Mark Latimer's lies, too shattered by his own disillusion, too eaten up with jealous rage to question them.

He was appalled at his own blindness, at the way he had failed her, seeing himself as the injured party. And all the time she had seen his lack of support as proof that he, like everyone else, had found what she had done unforgivable. And it couldn't have helped that everything he'd said to her since finding her here at Vine House had confirmed her in that belief. When he remembered some of his accusations he wished he could cut out his tongue.

The scars on her body had shocked him, tearing at his heart and filling him with a helpless anger, yet the mental and emotional scars were even more terrible, and the knowledge that he had inflicted some of those himself was insupportable. There *had* to be a way he could reach her, convince her she didn't have to go on paying for the rest of her life for that one tragic action. He'd failed her once, but now fate was giving him a second chance, and this time he meant to grasp it with both hands.

At that moment Siriol surfaced beside him in the water. Her face alive with laughter she swept the wet hair out of her eyes with her hands. But as the sun glinted on the diamond he had put on her finger only a short time ago, Fraser found it impossible to smile back.

As Bethan entered the house from the garden, Molly Flowerdew was just admitting Dr Stratton at the front door. Alarmed that something had happened while she had been at the pool, she hurried forward. 'Lorna— she's not fallen or something?'

'No, my dear no one's called me out,' the doctor hastened to assure her. 'This is more of a social call. I thought it would be pleasant to put my feet up here for half an hour, especially if Molly can produce some of her delicious scones.' He cocked an eye at the housekeeper who beamed back at him.

'You take the doctor through to the sitting-room, Miss Bethan. I'll have them scones buttered in five minutes.' Molly hurried away to the kitchen.

'You've been in the pool, I see.' For all his balding head and growing paunch, the doctor eyed Bethan's long slim legs appreciatively.

Half expecting his disapproval she said defensively, 'Mr Laurie has already taken me to task for swimming alone.'

'Has he now? Well, I'd say you've got a sensible head on your shoulders and I reckon you wouldn't have gone in if you hadn't felt up to it,' was his disarming reply. 'Though maybe it isn't a good idea to hang around too long in those wet clothes. Come and join us when you've changed.' He stumped towards the sitting-room and Bethan obediently ran up the stairs.

It took her no longer than ten minutes to shower and dress so when she returned to the sitting-room she was surprised to see Fraser, his dark hair gleaming damply, sitting with his aunt and the doctor, and Siriol nowhere in evidence. She was very much aware of his grey eyes raking over her as she entered the room quietly, though she couldn't read their expression, and she hoped very much his appearance at tea didn't mean he and his fiancée had quarrelled.

Molly brought in the tea-trolley and the conversation was general as they all tucked into her scones and the light sponge cake that melted on the tongue.

'I can see both my patients are recovering their appetite.' For all his own apparent dedication to Molly's delicacies, Dr Stratton had been watchful. 'In fact I'd say Lorna in particular has picked up marvellously again.'

'Thanks to Bethan.' Lorna's blue eyes twinkled at her fondly. 'She looks after me like a daughter, bullies me so gently into obeying orders I don't even know she's doing it most of the time.'

Bethan flushed, denying the accolade. 'But I've done

so little. In fact half the time you've had to look after *me*, Lorna, and I feel bad about that.' She could feel Fraser's eyes on her, accusingly she was sure, though she couldn't bring herself to look.

'And maybe that's what's wrought the miracle,' Dr Stratton said thoughtfully. 'You've made her feel needed, Bethan, given her a purpose, something to get well for.'

'And maybe you're right at that,' Lorna laughed. 'Whatever the cause I *do* feel better. Oh, my hip still pains me of course, but I certainly seem to have recovered my energy.'

'And that's all we've been waiting for.' The doctor leaned back in his chair, eyeing Lorna approvingly. 'I think I can at last begin to set things in motion for your operation, my dear.'

'But is my aunt really strong enough to face that yet?' Fraser demanded, and something in his voice had them all looking at him curiously. 'There's no sense in rushing things while she has Bethan here to make sure she doesn't slip back.'

'But my dear boy, *you* were the one who talked me into agreeing to have the operation in the first place, to get me mobile again.' Lorna looked at him with amused bewilderment. '*You* were the one who advocated the least possible delay, nagging me night and day to have a nurse to get me well again as quickly as possible. And I *am* well again. In fact I'm feeling more vigorous than I have done in years.' Seeing her sparkling eyes and teasing smile, Bethan could believe it. She had put on a little weight too, filling out the floral silk dress she wore much better than she had done when Bethan first arrived at Vine House.

'All right.' Fraser made a capitulating gesture. 'Of course I want to see you walking without pain again, Lorna. And if you're sure you feel up to it ...' His steely gaze lanced unexpectedly at Bethan. 'Just as long as Bethan doesn't see the operation as a signal for her to go rushing back to work for the relief agency.'

'But of course she mustn't,' Lorna said at once. 'I wouldn't dream of letting her go before she's fully fit.'

'No need to worry on that score,' Dr Stratton said comfortably. 'It'll be two or three weeks before the arrangements are complete to get Lorna admitted to hospital, say three weeks before she's home again, and I'm sure she'll be glad of her nurse's services for a couple of weeks after that. That gives us another two months to get Bethan up to strength again, ample time at the rate of progress she's making.'

'Two months! You really think two months is going to make her fit enough to face all that again—the killing climate, privations, disease, semi-starvation, not to mention stray bombs and bullets?' Fraser spoke with a barely restrained violence, a whiteness round his mouth.

Bethan sat rigid in her chair, her hands clasped fiercely together in her lap, aware of Lorna's surprise at her nephew's outburst turning to speculation as her bright blue eyes flicked from Fraser to Bethan and back again. 'I'm sure you're right,' Lorna agreed. 'We must do all we can to persuade her to stay on. Perhaps you and Siriol could take her out sometimes, introduce her to some of the younger folk around here. If she meets a nice young man . . .'

Bethan's cheeks burned, because Lorna seemed to be telling her not to read too much into Fraser's concern, reminding her that he was engaged to be married and so was not free to show too much interest in her—Bethan's—welfare. Remembering Fraser's appalled expression when he had seen her scars, Bethan wanted to reassure his aunt she need have no fears on that score; that any concern Fraser displayed was only prompted by pity, but Dr Stratton was already rising reluctantly from his chair to take his leave.

'Well, the longer you can persuade Nurse Steele to stay the better.' he said, 'Though I'm happy with her progress. Keep up the swimming, my dear. A bit of gentle exercise will give you a healthy appetite. Do you ride? It's a very good way of seeing more of the countryside while you're here without overtaxing yourself.'

'I—I used to,' Bethan admitted. 'But it's a long time ago, and I don't know if there are any riding stables around here.'

'I can find a mount for you,' Fraser said tersely, following the doctor out of the room and leaving Bethan staring after him.

He didn't return to the sitting-room to enlarge on his offer and after time for thought Bethan hoped he might forget it. She wished he hadn't caught her at the pool earlier, wished even more fervently she hadn't been shaken into talking to him of things she had never spoken of to anyone before. It had altered things between them in some indefinable way. Much as his earlier antagonism had disturbed her, it had been easier to fight than his pity. Any show of concern from him weakened her defences against him, making it all too easy to deceive herself into believing he might return the feelings that sometimes threatened to overwhelm her, when all she knew of him told her loud and clear that it was only wishful thinking. And even if he *had* felt some small measure of the attraction that drew her so inexorably to him, she told herself firmly, it couldn't make any difference. Both their lives were mapped out, his with Siriol, the wife he had chosen, hers paying off the debt for the life she had destroyed. Much better that for the remaining weeks of her enforced stay at Vine House she should see as little of him as possible.

But after she had helped Lorna change for dinner and had slipped on another of her clean but worn cotton shirts, she accompanied her employer downstairs again, to find both Fraser and Siriol waiting for them in the sitting-room. Siriol looked very pretty and very much the rich man's daughter in a floor-length chiffon dress of glowing red that exposed a tantalising amount

of tanned and well-rounded young shoulders. But it was
to Fraser that Bethan's eyes were irresistibly drawn, his
light grey trousers and matching tailored shirt em-
phasising his brooding darkness, and when for several
breathless seconds his eyes met and held hers it was like
leaving something of herself behind when she tore her
gaze away and helped Lorna into her chair. Lorna too,
though not as formally dressed as Siriol, had made
some concession to evening wear, and Bethan couldn't
help feeling consciously shabby in her plain cotton
knee-length skirt that was her only alternative to
trousers, and after settling Lorna comfortably she
selected a chair outside their charmed circle as Fraser
moved lithely from the drinks tray to hand his aunt her
glass of sherry.

'Won't you let me get you a drink, Bethan?' He
turned to her persuasively. 'Sherry ... martini ...
perhaps a glass of our own wine?'

'Thank you, no.' Bethan shook her head firmly and
was surprised to see the angry tightening of his mouth.

'One small drink isn't likely to send you off the rails
again, you know,' he grated in a voice too low for the
others to hear, but when Bethan flinched, her eyes
stricken, he muttered, 'Oh hell! I'm sorry . . .'

'Is my fiancé telling you off again, Bethan? Come and
sit over here by me, I'll protect you.' Siriol patted the
sofa at her side but her smile was strained, her voice
slightly too high to be natural. Darting a wary glance at
Fraser, Bethan did as she asked.

'I understand Dr Stratton's given the okay for Aunt
Lorna's operation to go ahead,' Siriol went on, and
again Bethan found herself glancing at Fraser,
wondering if he had confided in his fiancée his initial
inexplicable opposition to the operation. 'Does that
mean you'll be leaving us soon to go back to the relief
agency?'

Bethan couldn't help but be aware of the hope in the
other girl's voice, even as she was aware of Fraser's

dark brooding gaze on her though she couldn't bring herself to meet it.

'It'll be a few weeks yet, but yes, as soon as Lorna's fully recovered again,' she said quietly.

'I'll have to let the rest of my family know as soon as Dr Stratton's given me a date,' Lorna herself joined in.

'I've already telephoned Ishbel this evening.' Fraser tossed off the rest of his whisky. 'I wanted to give her time to arrange things to be here.'

Lorna looked amazed. 'Ishbel! Fraser dear, much as I'd love to see her, surely she doesn't think it necessary to come all the way from Australia on *my* account? It's not as if I'm *ill.*'

'Sorry to disillusion you, my love.' Fraser was attempting to keep the whole thing light but not quite succeeding. 'It isn't entirely on your account.' He walked across to the drinks tray and replenished his glass and Bethan noticed he spilt some as if his hand was not quite steady. 'I told my sister you were here,' he went on, turning back to face Bethan directly. 'She's very keen to see you before you disappear into the blue again.'

Bethan's startled eyes tried to read his expression that seemed to register little beyond a grim determination. And before she could fully assimilate the news that her old friend apparently lived now in Australia and that she was prepared to come all the way back to England just so they could meet, Siriol was saying with a surprise that was almost accusing, 'Bethan *knows* your sister?'

There was an oddly charged silence that Bethan hurried to fill. 'Ishbel and I were at school together, Siriol, but we lost touch when——' she hesitated and settled for the least complicated explanation, '——when I took up nursing. I didn't even know she lived in Australia.'

'She married an Aussie—Grant Shuster—and helps him run a vineyard many times the size of this one.'

Fraser had come to stand in front of her so she had to crane her neck to look up at him. He went on deliberately, 'It's been a very successful marriage, they're very happy. They have two small boys whom Ishbel intends to bring with her on this trip, even if Grant can't make it.'

Bethan's green eyes widened and a tinge of colour stained her cheeks. Was he trying to make her envious of Ishbel's good fortune? Remembering telling him only that afternoon that the things other women took for granted—a husband and family—were not for her, it seemed very much like it. But she wouldn't give him the satisfaction of knowing his jibe had hurt.

'I'm very glad Ishbel found the right man,' she said softly. 'I never did believe she was really in love with my stepbrother. She only imagined it because——' she broke off just in time, realising she had been about to say, 'because she knew I was in love with you,' and amended it to, 'because she was only in love with love.'

'But if you knew Ishbel, you must have known Fraser too!' Siriol broke in, looking from one to the other. 'And yet that first night after you came home, Fraser, you behaved as if Bethan was a stranger.'

And a stranger he didn't at all like, Bethan remembered tensely. His antagonism that first night had been obvious to everyone. 'You must remember I was still a child when I used to go to Merrifields.' She forced a smile for Siriol. 'You really couldn't expect him to remember the carroty-haired brat who used to pester him.'

Siriol's dark eyes still registered doubt as she turned them up to her fiancé. 'But you *did* remember her, didn't you, Fraser?' she said with uncanny perception. 'So why did you try to make us believe you didn't?'

Bethan was aware that Lorna too was waiting for Fraser's answer, and though she would have liked to help him out of a difficult spot her tongue seemed stuck to the roof of her mouth.

'There had been—misunderstandings,' Fraser said at last. 'Over the way we lost touch with Bethan. And that's why Ishbel's so keen to get here to see her now.'

His answer relieved the tension, and though Bethan was sure Siriol was curious to know what those 'misunderstandings' had been, she wisely didn't ask, and happily Molly arrived just then with the dinner-trolley.

That night Bethan slept heavily, more tired than she'd been since her collapse by the time she got to bed after a day that seemed to have been loaded with tension. Though the conversation had moved to safer topics with the arrival of the meal, Bethan had all too often been conscious of Fraser's darkly brooding gaze on her, yet every time her own eyes had been drawn to him he had been looking elsewhere.

But in spite of sleeping so heavily she was awake very early the next morning, and unable to lie in bed, she showered and dressed. There was no mist portending another hot day this morning, only grey skies and a wind that tossed tendrils of honeysuckle and rambler-rose against her window-pane. Shivering, Bethan pulled on her cotton jacket over her shirt and wished that on her one trip to Framlingham in her first week at Vine House she had bought something warmer to wear.

She was brushing her hair, believing herself to be the only one stirring in the house when she was surprised by a brief knock on her door before it opened. While she still stared at him open-mouthed, Fraser, fully dressed in dark cord hip-hugging trousers and a thick Aran sweater, said casually, 'Oh good, you're ready, I see.'

Her temper spurted. For all he'd known or cared she might have been half-naked when he'd burst in! 'I'm *dressed*, luckily,' she responded tartly. 'But what I'm supposed to be ready for, I'm afraid I can't guess.'

His eyes gleamed but the mockery in them was softened as his mouth curved in a heart-stopping grin.

'Why, to go riding, of course. Didn't we arrange it yesterday?'

He knew damn well they'd arranged nothing after he'd thrown out his terse offer, but the thought of being on horseback again was enough to subdue her angry retort. 'Riding? You really meant it, then?' Unknowingly her face lit up with eagerness.

'Of course I meant it.' His eyes raked over her as she stood up and came towards him. 'You'll need something warmer to wear than that, though.'

'Oh, I'm sure I'll be all right when I get going,' she claimed, seeing her treat being withdrawn when she had to admit to his implacable expression, 'I don't have anything else.'

'Nonsense, you must have.' Impatiently he strode to her wardrobe and snatched open the door, his mouth tightening when his disbelieving gaze took in the paucity of the few shabby garments hanging there. 'Is this all?' He broke off as, riffling through them, he came to the silk caftan. 'And how did *this* exotic garment stray in here?'

His voice had hardened as if all his earlier suspicion of her was back, and yet why? she wondered, inexplicably wounded, when his fiancée's wardrobe must contain dozens of far more expensive and elaborate dresses than that?

She lifted her chin. 'Impractical, isn't it? But it was generously meant. I found it in the luggage that was sent back from Beirut after I was injured, a get-well present from my colleagues there.'

A trace of colour stained Fraser's cheekbones as he put the caftan back wordlessly, making no attempt to apologise for the nasty thoughts she knew had been crossing his mind. 'You don't even have a sweater?' he asked, closing the wardrobe door.

'You've seen everything I own,' she snapped, still annoyed with him, 'unless you wish to examine my underwear.'

'Is that an invitation, Bethan?' He advanced towards her, a wicked gleam in his eyes, and she backed away, disconcerted by his sudden change of mood.

'In the drawer, I meant,' she amended hastily, and swallowed hard as, still advancing on her he began to peel off his heavy sweater. Surely he didn't mean to— His devilish grin told her he had read her thoughts as he held the sweater out to her.

'Sorry to disappoint you, but far from *un*dressing you I was going to suggest you borrow this.'

'I—I didn't—I wasn't——' she choked helplessly, her cheeks flaming. She had seen him in many moods, hostile, accusing, even pitying, and after his suspicions of only moments ago, this sudden switch to *flirtatiousness* threw her into utter confusion.

The soft wool of his sweater brushed against her hands but he didn't release his hold on it, dropping it himself over her head, smiling as it swamped her, though he couldn't know what it was doing to her, feeling it still warm from the heat of his body, impregnated with the intoxicating male smell of him. She stood like a puppet, fighting her senses as he folded up the long sleeves to let her hands emerge and turned down the heavy rollneck to free her chin, and the sudden descent of his mouth on hers took her utterly by surprise, too stunned by the sheer unexpectedness of it to either respond or reject him.

He drew back, a strange, unreadable expression on his face. 'Anyone would think you'd never been kissed since the last time *I* kissed you ten years ago,' he said harshly, no lightness in his mood now.

Still too stunned to move, the expression on her suddenly burning face gave her away.

'My God! I don't believe you have! Bethan——'

He was coming too close to discovering her true feelings and convulsively she pulled away from him. 'I told you before,' she said flatly. 'There's been no room in my life for such things.'

For one heart-stopping moment she thought he was going to drag her back into his arms and prove her a liar, but he only grabbed her wrist and fairly dragged her out of the room.

She could still feel his anger when they reached the stables where the two horses were already saddled and waiting for them, but somehow she didn't feel that this time his anger was directed at her but rather at himself. And so it should be, she told herself, her own anger rising at his unprincipled behaviour. He had no right to flirt with her, much less kiss her, when he was engaged to marry Siriol Miles.

But in spite of the overcast morning she found she couldn't sustain her anger with the horse moving rhythmically beneath her and the cool wind in her hair. They skirted the perimeter of the vineyard, Fraser explaining how the vines had to be sprayed every two weeks against various pests and diseases that could attack them until they began to flower some time in July, when mildew would become the greatest menace, and how the young shoots had to be tied in as they grew to prevent them being snapped off by the wind. Bethan listened with interest, prompting him with questions of her own.

'I'd no idea there *were* any vineyards in Britain,' she confessed, 'so what gave you the idea of starting one?'

'Not me, Uncle Henry. Lorna's late husband,' he elucidated at her blank expression. 'And it's by no means the only one. Vines were grown in England back in Roman times and continued to be cultivated through history—though they received a set-back at the dissolution of the monasteries in the sixteenth century—until the First World War killed them off. It was just after the last war that two enterprising gentlemen—a Mr Barrington-Brock and a Mr Hyams—started the revival of viticulture in England, and since then there's been a tremendous upsurge of interest. There must be getting on for two hundred commercial vineyards in this country now, not to mention I don't know how many private ones. Research into new varieties of vines suitable to our climate has made it a much less dicey business than it once was.'

'I suppose it must be a profitable undertaking for you to devote your time to it.' She was aware of the mocking look he slanted at her and flushed. 'Well, I seem to remember the farm at Merrifields was very prosperous. You wouldn't have given that up unless——'

'Who says I've given it up?'

Her flush deepened. 'I'm sorry. I thought——' She broke off in embarrassed confusion, then apologised again. 'I'm sorry, it's none of my business.'

Fraser ignored her disclaimer. 'All the Laurie interests are run centrally by Laurie Holdings Ltd, of which I'm the managing director. That includes the original farm at Merrifields, this vineyard, a deer-farm where we raise venison for the table and meat-distributing and exporting business. I also play a part in the promotion of English wines.'

'I—I see.' Bethan wondered why he was telling her all this. 'I don't suppose you can spend much time at Merrifields then.'

'No. My father and my uncle are semi-retired now and one of my cousins looks after the operation there. You won't find it changed much, though.'

He spoke as if there was the possibility of her seeing it again. Bethan knew nothing could be less likely and kept silent, the memory of her last visit there too painfully acute.

And as if he could see into her mind Fraser reached over and took her reins, forcing her to a stop. 'Bethan, for God's sake, what happened that night?' His voice was strained, something in his eyes as they searched her face almost like pain. 'I wouldn't believe them at first when they told me—thought there must be some confusion over names. Damn it, I'd never known you to drink, apart from the odd glass of sherry or wine, and I know Ishbel was only serving up an innocuous punch that night. And in any case you weren't the sort to let someone lead you into that kind of reckless stupidity as Ishbel might have been led. So what happened that particular night to make you hit the bottle? *Something* must have done to bring about such an uncharacteristic change.'

She was all too aware of the clasp of his hands, of his leg pressed hard up against hers as she sat rigid with tension. It was little comfort that he believed that one catastrophic bout of drunkenness was uncharacteristic, when the only explanation she had ever been able to come up with for her behaviour that night of Ishbel's party had been her misery at his rejection of her in the summer-house.

CHAPTER EIGHT

BETHAN shuddered. How could she tell him that? Everything in her revolted against allowing him to know just how deeply that long-ago rejection had hurt her, and anyway, he might think she was trying to excuse herself, shift the blame.

'I don't know.' The words came out on an agonised sigh. 'I don't remember *anything* about Ishbel's party.' And that was the truth, because she still had no recollection of anything that had happened after Fraser had left her in the summer-house to rejoin his girlfriend. 'I don't remember drinking anything, I don't remember taking Mark's car, I don't even remember hitting that child. It's all a blank until I woke up in hospital the next day with a policeman at my bedside, and they told me what I'd done.' She shuddered again and raised wide, haunted green eyes to his face. 'Don't you see, it seems to make what I did so much worse, because I can't remember.'

His hands tightened over hers in a crushing grip and the expression in his own eyes was almost as haunted. 'Bethan, it wasn't because of——'

She tensed, dreading the question she was sure was coming, then to her profound relief he released her hands and drew away. 'But if you can't remember . . .' He urged his horse on, but it was several moments before she could pull herself together sufficiently to follow.

The rest of the ride was completed in silence, Fraser seeming preoccupied with thoughts that from the expression on his face were not pleasant ones, and Bethan afraid that to remind him of her presence might provoke more unanswerable questions.

They had to pass the garage that housed Fraser's
Mercedes and Lorna's Rover to reach the stables, and
as if that sparked off a new train of thought Fraser said
abruptly as he dismounted, 'Do you still drive?'

'No!' Bethan shook her head.

'You've never driven since——?' Fraser stood
looking up at her, his reins looped over his arm.

'What do you think?' She looked away, her hands
gripping the front edge of the saddle tightly. 'Oh, there
have been occasions when I've *had* to drive—a Land
Rover out in the African bush—but nowhere where
there was a chance of doing anyone any harm.'

The hands that seized her round the waist were
strong and hard, and though she protested that she
would rather dismount unaided, he plucked her out of
the saddle as if she weighed no more than a child. And
though he didn't release her at once his grip slackened
as her feet touched the ground so that it would have
been easy for her to move away. Only, seduced by his
nearness, Bethan didn't move, *couldn't* move, could
hardly even breathe, trapped like a fly in the spider's
web of his attraction.

But when she dared to raise her eyes to his face, he
wasn't even looking at her but at something beyond her.

'Siriol, just the girl I want to see.' Fraser took the
reins from Bethan's nerveless fingers as she drew a long,
shuddering breath. 'You're going into Framlingham
this morning, aren't you? Will you take Bethan along
with you? She needs to buy some warmer clothes.'

His words and the faintly hostile way Siriol was
staring at her reminded Bethan she was still wearing
Fraser's sweater and she would have peeled it off on the
spot had he not forcibly restrained her. 'Not now, you
silly girl. Keep it on till you get back to the house. Do
you want to get a chill on top of everything else?'

Bethan looked at Siriol apologetically. 'It was very
kind of Fraser to lend it to me when I had nothing
warm enough to wear.'

Siriol nodded a stiff acknowledgment and turned at once to Fraser. 'You didn't tell me you were taking Bethan riding this morning.' Her voice betrayed her jealousy, and Bethan wanted to cry out that there was no need for it.

'A gentle amble to the bottom of the vineyard and back through Copp's Meadow? You don't call that a ride.' Fraser's eyes gleamed at Bethan mockingly and she knew he was remembering her hell-for-leather style of horsemanship of years ago when her only ambition had been to outstrip him. 'Both horses still have a gallop in them. Hop up, Siriol, and we'll let them stretch their legs up on the common.'

It was as if someone had turned a light on inside Siriol as she sprang lithely into the saddle Bethan had just vacated. 'Ten o'clock suit you, Bethan? I'll pick you up then. 'Bye.' Without waiting for an answer she cantered out of the yard, Fraser following close behind, leaving Bethan feeling unjustifiably lonely and forlorn.

The weather had brightened considerably by the time Siriol's small cream sports-car swept into the drive and tooted imperiously, though the brisk wind still drove scudding clouds across the sun from time to time. Siriol's buoyant mood at Fraser's invitation to ride with him seemed to have deserted her again, and the younger girl swung between forced cheerfulness and preoccupied silence on the drive through the lush country lanes. It was Saturday and the small market town was busy so they had to drive round the narrow streets before they found a space to park and eventually finished up near the castle.

Siriol recommended what she considered to be the best shop Framlingham had to offer, but with a doubtful glance at the younger girl's stylish linen dress and matching jacket, Bethan protested that she needed something warm and hard-wearing and definitely not expensive.

'Oh, I don't shop there myself,' Siriol admitted

blithely. 'At least, only occasionally for things like jeans and tights. But I'm sure they'll be able to fix you up.'

Smiling without rancour at her companion's unintentionally crushing remark, Bethan allowed herself to be overruled, and half an hour later she had selected a couple of sweaters—one thick and one much lighter—a pair of warmer trousers that would go with either of them and much more fashionably cut than any she already owned, and a woollen blazer-style jacket.

Siriol was riffling along a dress-rack while Bethan paid for her puchases and drew out a cotton sundress in a lovely shade of sea-green.

'Thinking of buying it?' Bethan asked.

'It's very pretty.' Siriol was looking at it covetously. 'Pity it's not my size. It would fit you, though, and it's just your colour.' She said it reluctantly, as if she regretted it as soon as the words were spoken.

It was indeed a pretty dress, but with both the back and the front scooped out low, Bethan knew it wasn't for her and shook her head regretfully. 'No, I don't think so, Siriol.'

Oddly Siriol looked pleased at her refusal to be tempted, and contrarily Bethan found herself wanting very much to have something pretty she could change into in the evenings. Her eyes travelled on along the rail, stopping at a black silk shirt. 'But something like this . . .' She reached it off the rail. 'This wouldn't put anyone off their food, would it?'

Of course Siriol didn't know what she was talking about and Bethan felt obliged to explain. 'My back was burned in that bomb blast, that's why I could never wear anything as revealing as that green dress.'

Siriol's mouth and eyes rounded, but before she could comment, the assistant, seeing another sale, said helpfully, 'There's a black skirt that'll go perfectly with that blouse.'

And it did, a skirt of fine Indian crimped cotton that clung to her hips but swirled around her legs as she

moved. 'My, that really does something for you!' The
assistant was back again, clasping a gold belt round her
waist and urging her into high-heeled black sandals.

Bethan stared at the woman reflected in the mirror
and it was like looking at a stranger, someone almost—
beautiful! The body of the blouse was opaque and hid
her disfigurement, but the full sleeves were of a fine
chiffon that revealed the gleam of her skin and the
plunging vee neckline was softened by ruffles of the
same fabric. A surge of amazed excitement brought a
glow to skin that looked almost opalescent against the
black and gave a glitter to her green eyes, while her halo
of hair looked as if it had been burnished.

Bethan found herself paying for her new finery in a
daze, unaware that Siriol had grown steadily more
silent. 'Now, what about *your* errands?' Bethan said as
they left the shop.

Siriol looked at her blankly for a moment as if her
thoughts had been elsewhere. 'Oh, that doesn't matter,'
she muttered. 'Let's have a coffee, shall we?'

She led the way to a nearby café but it was crowded
and they had to share a table, and Bethan had barely
time to drink her coffee before Siriol was urging her out
again and straight back to the car-park.

Her parcels safely in the boot, Bethan looked up at
the outer walls of the castle as she waited for Siriol to
unlock the passenger door, wishing she could have
explored it while she was so close and wondering what
was quaintly odd about it. And then she realised most of
the towers were topped by tall, decorated chimney-pots
that looked as if they dated back to Tudor times,
something she didn't recall having seen on a ruined
castle before.

But for all her hurry, Siriol made no attempt to start
the engine when at last Bethan was sitting beside her.
She sat gripping the steering-wheel staring straight
ahead, her young body so stiff with tension her
knuckles gleamed white. Bethan glanced at her

curiously, hesitant about breaking in on the other girl's preoccupation. 'Is there something wrong, Siriol?' she eventually asked. 'You seem worried about something.'

For several seconds Siriol sat unmoving as if she hadn't heard, then turning her head she looked directly at Bethan. 'Shouldn't I be?' she challenged, her dark eyes defensive, uncertain. It was only when she recognised Bethan's bewilderment as genuine that she hunched her shoulders, letting her defensive gaze fall to her hands where she began to twist her engagement ring.

'I'm sorry, maybe I've got things wrong,' she muttered. 'I *hope* I've got things wrong, only—Bethan, I've got to ask. Just what *was* there between you and Fraser when you knew him before?'

Bethan drew in an audible breath while the question seemed to echo and re-echo round her brain. '*Nothing!*' she got out at last in a strangled voice.

But Siriol seized on her hesitation, not realising Bethan had been too surprised and shaken to know quite how to answer. 'You don't really expect me to believe that, do you? I may be a lot younger than Fraser but I'm neither stupid nor blind. He—he's different since you came here, sort of edgy, *angry* even. At first I thought it was because he didn't like you, but lately ...' There was a despairing catch in her voice. 'He hardly seems to see me any more when you're there. He——'

Bethan knew she had to stop this. Putting a hand on the other girl's arm she said fiercely, 'Don't! Believe me, you're upsetting yourself over nothing. Fraser's *never* thought of me in the way you seem to imagine.'

'Am I imagining it?' Siriol looked very young and defenceless as she searched Bethan's face. 'Are you honestly saying there was never anything between you and Fraser?'

Bethan's first impulse was to give the girl the assurance she wanted, to deny that Fraser had ever been more to her than her best friend's brother. But

Siriol wasn't a fool. She had already picked up the tension that Bethan couldn't deny existed between herself and the man Siriol was going to marry. If no more damage was to be done then Siriol deserved the truth, however much her own pride might suffer.

'No, I can't deny it,' she said quietly, and seeing Siriol flinch she went on firmly. 'But I can assure you that whatever there was between us was entirely on my side. I was very young, Siriol, younger than you are now, and I'd hero-worshipped Fraser since I was thirteen years old, so it wasn't really so surprising that I fell in love with him.'

'And Fraser?' Siriol said tensely. 'Did he——?'

Bethan took a deep breath to armour herself against a truth that could still hurt. 'Fraser wasn't very kind. He made it absolutely clear he preferred far more sophisticated ladies, glamorous models usually.'

'I—I see.' Siriol's eyes were wide and searching but there was sympathy and understanding there too. 'He must have hurt you very much,' she said quietly. 'And you still love him, don't you?'

Bethan wanted to deny it, but the betraying colour crept up her cheeks. Had she really been so obvious? 'Perhaps you should call it a case of arrested development,' she suggested drily. 'When you come a cropper off a horse the answer is to get straight back on again to restore your confidence. Perhaps if things had been different and I'd been in a position to fall in love with someone else I'd have got him out of my system, but there's been no room in my life these last ten years for relationships with men. So you see, Siriol, there's no cause for you to worry. Fraser didn't return my feelings then, and he certainly doesn't now.'

She hoped the humbling of her pride would be enough to reassure Siriol but there was still a lurking doubt in the younger girl's face. 'I wish I could be sure of that, Bethan, but I've seen the way he looks at you.'

'You're mistaken.' Bethan was remembering again

Fraser's appalled expression when he had seen her scars. 'He feels sorry for me, nothing more than that. He knows I ruined my life with one stupid, irresponsible act.'

And still Siriol didn't seem satisfied. 'He said there had been misunderstandings,' she ventured. 'I wondered——'

Did Siriol want to strip her of everything, her pride and her self-respect? Bethan wondered. There were some things she *couldn't* tell her. 'It's a long story and not really relevant any more. But yes, someone did make mischief,' she admitted warily. 'And Fraser knows the truth now. But those misunderstandings couldn't have happened in the first place if he'd cared at all for me. I accepted that long ago.'

She leaned her head back against the seat and closed her eyes to conceal just how painful that acceptance had been—still was. But she was unable to conceal the strain in her fine-drawn features or the trembling of her vulnerable mouth.

'I'm sorry if I've upset you, Bethan,' Siriol said uncertainly. 'It's just that I've been so afraid you were going to take Fraser from me.'

Slow anger began to churn through Bethan. Why couldn't Siriol have spoken to Fraser about her fears? He would have demolished them quickly enough. Did the girl have no imagination? No pity? She'd already forced Bethan into admitting she still loved Fraser, so couldn't she see how unfair it was to ask her for the reassurance she craved?

And then the anger died to be replaced by a painful compassion. Siriol was head over heels in love with Fraser, and loving him so much herself, Bethan could identify with the other girl's uncertainty and pain.

'Siriol, I couldn't take him away from you even if I wanted to,' she said wearily. 'And I *don't* want to. It's been—hard, meeting Fraser again, seeing him happy with someone else. But I'm glad it's someone like you.

The girl he once preferred to me—well, let's just say I don't think she would have made him happy, whereas I'm sure you will.'

'Oh Bethan, you don't know how I had to screw up my courage to have this talk with you, but I'm glad I did.' Impulsively Siriol leaned across and hugged her. 'You're nice, and I hated feeling jealous of you.'

Bethan knew exactly what she meant because she had struggled with the same feelings herself, and must go on struggling with them. 'It's Fraser you should have talked to about your fears,' she said drily. 'He'd soon have told you how needless they were.'

'You're probably right.' Siriol switched on the ignition and reversed out of the parking-space, her mood ebullient again. 'Trouble is,' she admitted wryly, 'I'm still a bit in awe of him. I mean, he's not the kind of man one can take one's troubles to, is he?'

Bethan stared at her in astonishment. Hadn't she spent her own teenage years doing just that, taking her troubles to Fraser and finding comfort? How much more easily should Siriol have been able to confide in him, loving him as she did and in a position to expect his loyalty? She told herself that Siriol was still very young and for all her veneer of sophistication, not as sure of herself as she liked to pretend.

She felt quite wrung out by the time Siriol dropped her off at Vine House and would have welcomed time to herself to regain her composure, but Lorna was lying in wait for her, demanding to see her purchases.

'Oh, I'm so glad you bought something pretty, Bethan,' she exclaimed delightedly when she saw the black skirt and blouse with its gold accessories. 'It'll be just the thing for you to wear tonight. Siriol's father is coming to dinner.' Her eyes twinkled. 'A charming man, but the kind one rather likes to keep one's end up with, if you know what I mean.'

Bethan wasn't sure if she liked the sound of that and looked so apprehensive that Lorna laughed. 'Oh dear, now you're imagining some kind of ogre, and I didn intend that at all. Don't worry, my dear, you have ju the kind of natural, inbred elegance that will appeal him, and wearing that new outfit you'll have him eatin out of your hand.'

Bethan shook her head disbelievingly, but later whe they were both ready to go down to dinner, Lorn triumphant, having insisted on seating Bethan at h dressing-table to add a touch of make-up to comple the transformation her new outfit made to h appearance, she felt a stirring of uneasiness as sl stared back at the unfamiliar image in the mirror. Th morning Siriol had bared her heart, desperately seekir reassurance that Bethan did *not* have designs on h fiancé. Bethan still knew she had neither the will nor tl power to steal Fraser's affections, but would Siri believe that? Wouldn't she wonder that Betha appeared to have made a special effort to loo attractive tonight?

But they were doubts she was unable to share wit Lorna and she had no alternative but to give h employer her arm to help her from the room. It wa unfortunate that just as they reached the turn in tl stairs, Fraser should be at the door admitting the guests. They all three looked up, Fraser's hanc arrested in the process of helping his fiancée off wit her fur jacket. The expressions in those three pairs c eyes were varied: Siriol, as Bethan had feared, looke shocked and accusing, while the thickset, grey-haire man at her side betrayed the fact that he had expecte something far different. But it was the expression c Fraser's face that held her riveted gaze, an expressio she had seen there only once before, that night in th summer-house at Merrifields when he had slid th straps of her dress from her shoulders and gazed at he naked breasts.

It was Lorna who broke the spell that bound ther all. 'George! How nice to see you again.' She held ou her hands in welcome as Bethan helped her down the remaining steps.

Bethan hung back as the old friends greeted each other and Fraser continued his interrupted movement of lifting the fur from Siriol's bare shoulders, but then Lorna was calling, 'Bethan, my dear, come and be introduced. This is Siriol's father, George Miles.'

Watching Siriol clutching Fraser's arm possessively, she was glad to turn away to the girl's father, only to find herself held in his assessing stare, eyes as dark as his daughter's but infinitely harder.

'Ah, the little nurse.' George Miles took her outstretched hand in a crushing grip, the heavy gold ring on his fourth finger biting into her flesh.

'How do you do, Mr Miles,' she responded with more composure than she felt, suspecting his greeting had been calculated to put her in her place.

The painful pressure on her hand slackened but he didn't release her, confounding her by saying jovially, 'Oh call me George, or are you trying to make me feel past being able to appreciate a beautiful woman by being so formal? You're a sly dog, Fraser, not letting on what a little stunner you've been harbouring under your roof.'

Fraser looked unaccountably angry and Bethan was at a loss to know how to handle this middle-aged man's gallantry, which was both heavy-handed and un-expected. It was Lorna who came to her rescue.

'Stop flirting with Bethan, George. She's much too wise to be taken in by it.'

George grinned at his hostess. 'You're only jealous. And *you* can stop glowering at me too, Fraser. I've given you my daughter so don't begrudge me this small consolation.' He gave Bethan's hand a final bone-crushing squeeze before releasing her at last and offering his arm to Lorna, escorting her to her chair in the sitting-room. But it was Bethan he chose to sit beside on one of the sofas, much too close for her

comfort, plying her with flowery compliments until she
squirmed with embarrassment.

The chaffing from his father-in-law-to-be had not
improved Fraser's expression, and he dispensed the
drinks still glowering. Bethan tried not to look at him
but even staring down at her hands clasped nervously in
her lap he filled her vision. Formally dressed tonight he
seemed bigger and more devastatingly attractive than
ever, his dark dinner-jacket fitting snugly across his
broad shoulders, the strong column of his neck looking
even more deeply tanned against the blue whiteness of
his pleated shirtfront.

She stole a glance at him to find him looking at her,
his grey eyes angry, his jaw set. 'Bethan, perhaps you'd
be good enough to fetch some more ice,' he suggested
coldly.

Scrambling to her feet she was glad to escape to
the kitchen, discovering only when she got there that
the ice bucket he had handed her was still more than
half full. She lingered in the kitchen as long as she
dared, relieved to see the dinner was almost ready to
be served.

When she returned to the sitting-room she pretended
not to see George Miles pat the seat beside him
invitingly. 'The dinner-trolley's on its way,' she said
quietly to Lorna. 'Perhaps you'd like me to help you get
to the table.'

She was pleased to find herself seated between Lorna
and Fraser, looking out on to the still sunlit garden,
and under the influence of Molly's superb cooking the
atmosphere became more convivial, George Miles
ceasing his heavy-handed flirtation in favour of more
general conversation and Fraser losing his glowering
expression and responding while Siriol sparkled between
the pair of them. Bethan slowly began to relax. Perhaps
this awful evening wasn't going to turn out too badly
after all.

She looked across interestedly when Siriol said, 'I

hope you won't be going into hospital before the midsummer party, Lorna. You just *have* to be there.'

'As it's not for another couple of weeks there's every chance I *shall* miss it this year,' Lorna grimaced. 'But you'll be able to go, Bethan.' She brightened up immediately. 'You'll love it. George and Siriol throw their house open and people come from far and wide. It's become quite a tradition since they moved into the Old Vicarage. The Saturday night nearest to Midsummer Day.'

Everything in Bethan shied away from the idea. She didn't want to spend yet another evening watching Siriol and Fraser together, building up the traditions that would make up their lives. It was too painful. Neither did she want to give George Miles another opportunity to pay her his unwelcome attentions.

'If you're able to go then of course I'll be glad to go with you,' she said quietly. 'But I couldn't go alone.'

'Nonsense, my dear, of course you can,' Lorna declared. 'You won't be alone anyway. Fraser will take you.'

'Of course,' Fraser agreed, his voice expressionless.

'Oh no.' Bethan glanced at him quickly and away again, feeling the tension rising tangibly between them and noticing that neither Siriol nor her father were adding their persuasions. 'Fraser will be there with Siriol,' she said to Lorna, 'which is as it should be. Parties aren't in my line, Lorna. I'd be embarrassed not knowing anyone.'

'But that's why I want you to go,' Lorna wailed. 'It'll be an opportunity for you to meet some young people, make some friends. And if I have to miss all the fun, how am I going to hear about it unless you tell me? Fraser certainly won't. He never notices the important things.'

'Like who's wearing what and who's gossiping about whom,' Fraser put in slyly. 'Give in gracefully, Bethan, and spare me *that* particular cross-examination. It's not

as if you have the excuse you've nothing to wear. It'll b
a chance to give that lovely silk caftan hanging in you
wardrobe an airing.'

The sudden silence was deafening, and mortifie
colour rose up Bethan's neck and flooded her cheeks a
she could hear the other three people at the tabl
speculating how Fraser knew what she had in he
wardrobe.

'Well, if you already have something to wear.' Lorn
broke the silence. 'Though I was rather looking forwar
to taking you shopping to buy something spectacular.'

'This *is* pretty spectacular,' Fraser said drily, as i
unaware of the speculation his remark had caused.

Her face as white now as it had been scarlet moment
ago, Bethan lifted her chin. 'It was a get-well presen
from my colleagues at the hospital in Beirut,' sh
explained to the table at large. 'I happened to commen
to Fraser that, lovely as it is, a warm sweater woul
have been more practical.'

As an explanation of Fraser's remark she knew i
wasn't terribly convincing, but she was relieved to se
some of the jealous uncertainty fade from Siriol's face
The girl's father, though, was still studying her wit
hard, sceptical eyes.

Bethan's hands were still shaking when they returne
to the sitting-room for coffee and Lorna asked her to
hand out the cups. She was bending over the tray and
didn't see Fraser come up behind her on the pretext o
helping, so when he said in an undertone, 'Bethan, I'm
sorry if I embarrassed you,' she was startled into
looking up at him.

The mixture of expressions she saw in his face held
her transfixed; frustration, a kind of hunted anger, and
strangest of all, something that might have been
tenderness. That, and the note of genuine contrition in
his voice undermined her defences and unknowingly her
delicate features mirrored all her hurt and longing.

There was an answering flare in Fraser's grey eyes

before they darkened and the comfortable sitting-room
with the rest of its occupants receded. The very air
seemed to pulsate around them as she was caught in the
forcefield of his magnetism, held as immovably as iron
to a lodestone.

George Miles's voice reached her as if from a
distance. 'Now Lorna's operation is set to go ahead,
maybe it's time we fixed a date for the wedding eh,
Fraser? Especially as I understand your sister's coming
over from Australia. Couldn't be a better time to have
it than while she's here.'

Fraser's jaw clenched and what looked like sheer fury
blazed momentarily from his eyes, but it was gone so
quickly as he turned towards his prospective father-in-
law that Bethan knew she must have been mistaken.

'Changed your tune, haven't you, George?' he said
mildly. 'Two months ago you were insisting we waited
six months to be sure Siriol knew her own mind.' He
calmly carried coffee-cups to his aunt and his fiancée.

'You mean *you've* changed your mind, Daddy?' Siriol
gasped delightedly. 'You're not going to make us wait?'

Bethan bent her head over the tray again, wishing
herself anywhere but here, a captive listener to a
conversation that was deeply painful to her, but George
Miles's indulgent voice boomed out. 'I'll grant I had a
few misgivings, puss, wondering if you weren't letting
yourself be dazzled by the attentions of a sophisticated
older man.' He took the cup Fraser held out to him,
and although the tone of his voice was still indulgent,
Bethan glimpsed the hardness in his eyes. 'But Siriol's
convinced me she really does know what she wants, so
I'm withdrawing that condition, my boy.'

'Daddy!' With a squeal of delight Siriol threw herself
at her father and hugged him. 'Oh Daddy, thank you.
Isn't that marvellous, Fraser?' She looked up at him,
her face flushed, her eyes sparkling with excitement.
'We can get married straight away!'

Bethan didn't think she could stand any more. She

had actually picked up the coffee-pot as an excuse to get herself out of the room to refill it before Fraser spoke. 'When you say straight away, are you contemplating an unseemly dash to the nearest register office?' he asked sardonically. 'What about your plans for a big splash—white lace and orange-blossom, a bevy of bridesmaids and a marquee on the lawn?'

Siriol looked dashed as if these things meant a lot to her, but her father said easily, 'It'll be in church and everything can be exactly as Siriol wants it. What's the use of having money if you can't make folks dance to the tune of it? Of course we'll still need time to arrange things—say six weeks, perhaps. Lorna will be out of hospital by then, your sister should still be here and so will your little friend.' His hard gaze flicked to Bethan. 'As she's an old family friend she wouldn't want to miss your wedding.'

Flinching, Bethan put the coffee-pot back on the tray with a bump. Of course she had known all along Fraser and Siriol would be married some time in the near future, but she had assumed it wouldn't be until after she had returned to her old life with the relief agency, when she would have too much to occupy her to allow herself to think about it. She certainly had never imagined she would have to witness it herself. A creeping coldness gripped her, a sense of being cut off for ever from the source of all warmth.

'I'm sure your money talks as loud as the next man's, George,' Fraser said smoothly, 'but there are other considerations.'

George Miles's eyes narrowed. 'Name one.'

'I can name at least four.' Fraser's head came up challengingly and Bethan wondered why he wasn't as eager as Siriol was to avail himself of her father's change of heart. Perhaps he didn't like to feel he was being manipulated. 'In the first place, Lorna hasn't even been given the date for her admission into hospital yet, so I doubt very much if she'll be up to the strain of attending a wedding in only six weeks' time.'

'Oh, you mustn't let *me* influence things, Fraser,' Lorna said at once. 'I could always use a wheel-chair if I can't make it under my own steam.'

'That's one objection out of the way,' George grunted.

'Secondly, it's highly unlikely my sister can extend her visit for so long this time,' Fraser went on as if neither of them had spoken. 'Thirdly, six weeks will bring us right into the busiest time in the farming community, which will make it impossible for most of my family and friends to attend.'

'Your sister will stay on if you ask her to,' George barked, making no attempt to hide his displeasure. 'And your family and friends are all in a position to take *one* day off, however busy they are.' The tone of his voice changed, smooth but with an underlying threat. 'Or are you no longer in such pressing need of my backing for your drive to export venison to Germany?'

Not by the movement of a muscle did Fraser's face betray a reaction to the threat, or even that he had heard it, but having been on the receiving end more than once, Bethan recognised the waves of anger emanating from him by his stance. 'And fourthly,' he clipped out, 'and after that remark, George, by far the most important consideration, not only Siriol but I too need the full six months to be certain marriage is what we want.'

'Fraser!' Siriol couldn't have sounded more wounded if Fraser had physically struck her. 'Darling, you don't mean it!'

The aggression draining out of him, he raked both his hands through his hair and there was compassion in his face as he looked down at her. 'Siriol, you're young, highly intelligent and very beautiful,' he said gently. 'You have too much going for you that you need your father to *buy* you a husband.'

Siriol stared up at him in hurt bewilderment. 'I don't
know what you mean, Fraser.' Tears welled up in her
eyes. 'I love you, you know I do.'

Fraser hesitated, obviously affected by her tears, but
then shooting a hard glance at her father, he stepped
back. 'Siriol, this is neither the time nor the place.'

'I'm inclined to agree,' Lorna put in firmly. 'The date
of their wedding is something that should be decided by
the young people themselves, George without our
interference. Fraser, I think I should like a little brandy
with my coffee.'

'Far be it from me to interfere. I only wanted them to
know they don't have to wait if they don't want to.'
George Miles's voice was mild and conciliatory as he
stood up, but when he crossed the room to return his
cup to the tray, Bethan was sure he was feeling far from
conciliatory. She could understand his wish to see his
pretty daughter happy, but not his methods of
achieving that end. Did he really intend to withdraw his
backing from the business project if Fraser didn't do
as he wanted? And would Fraser eventually bow to that
pressure? Either way Bethan couldn't see it augured
well for Fraser's happiness. And though her heart ached
with the knowledge that inevitably their ways must
soon part again, she *did* want him to be happy.

'I'm afraid we've shocked Bethan with our little
argument.' George Miles was smiling at her, a smile
that didn't quite reach his eyes, and when he reached
out playfully to pat her cheek she had to steel herself
not to draw away. 'She's gone quite pale. What you
need, my dear, is a breath of fresh air. Come, you and I
will take a turn in the garden.' He leered at her. 'It's not
often I get the chance to stroll in the moonlight with a
pretty woman.'

Bethan recoiled from the idea of spending any time
alone with this man. His heavy-handed flirtatiousness
embarrassed her and she found his ruthlessness
frightening. But wouldn't she be doing Fraser and Siriol

favour if she distracted him for a while? It would have been better if the couple could have been persuaded to spend a little time together in the garden to make up their differences, but failing that, she could at least ensure George Miles didn't return to the offensive. So reluctantly she allowed him to tuck her hand into the crook of his arm and lead her out of the sitting-room, through the french window and into the garden.

But though his grip on her hand tightened when she would have drawn it away, he made no attempt to follow up his earlier flirtatious remarks as he led her along one of the paths, the scent of lavender and verbena rising up as her skirts brushed them. In fact he was silent until they reached the sundial in the centre of the knot-garden where he stopped, planting himself uncompromisingly in her path and forcing her to halt too. And there was none of his earlier gallantry in his voice when he demanded harshly, 'Well, Nurse Steele, how much do you want to take yourself off?'

The moon he had promised hung round and yellow over the vineyard and as it was almost midsummer there was still enough light to see clearly the pugnacious jut of his jaw and the ruthless gleam in his eyes. Bethan gasped. 'I *beg* your pardon?'

'I think I made myself perfectly clear,' he said insolently. 'How much is it going to cost me to persuasde you to go away and leave Fraser Laurie alone?'

Anger scorched through her at his brash insensitivity. Who did he think he was, to offer such an insult? As if money was the answer to everything, first trying to buy Fraser and now herself. Withering words rose to her tongue as she forced down the impulse to tell him just what he could do with his money, for some sixth sense told her she would be playing into his hands if she lost her temper.

Drawing away from him she said coldly, 'You can save your money, Mr Miles. Fraser isn't, and never has been, in any danger from me.'

'Don't play games with me, girlie.' He grasped he
arm, swinging her round as she made to move back t
the house. 'I've seen the way you give him the come-o
And I've seen him eating you with his eyes. You migl
have been lovers once, but he belongs to my girl now
so I'm telling you, hands off.'

Only by reminding herself that this man's distastefu
attack was prompted by his concern—misplaced thoug
it was—for his daughter's happiness, was Bethan abl
to hang on to her dignity. 'Fraser and I have *never* bee
lovers. He never saw me as anything more than hi
sister's schoolfriend. I doubt if he ever gave me so muc
as a passing thought in the ten years since I knew hi
before, and our meeting again now was purel
accidental. I'm sorry if my presence here has given yo
cause for concern, but believe me, you have no reaso
for it. As soon as I've seen Lorna through her operatio
I'll be going abroad again, back to my old job.'

'And in the meantime?' George Miles's eye
narrowed. 'Fraser won't break his engagement to marr
a penniless little nobody like *you*, you know. Lus
that's all it is, basic, old-fashioned lust. So why n
accept my offer and come out of this with cash in you
hand?'

Dear God, would this destructive encounter neve
end? Bethan was trembling and nauseous. 'I've tol
you, I don't want your money.' Her voice shoo
however hard she tried to control it. 'Neither have I an
desire to take Fraser away from Siriol, even if it wer
possible.'

'Do you think I was born yesterday?' he sneered. '
recognise a girl on the make when I see one. And n
man's going to turn down what's so blatantly offere
certainly not a man like Fraser. But I'm damned if I'
going to let you break my little girl's heart.' As h
spoke he glanced over her shoulder, back towards th
house, then his arms snaked out, dragging her agains
him. 'If you're so eager for a bit of fun to while awa

the monotony, why not try me? I can give you as good a time as *he* can.'

Even as she drew a breath to tell him what she thought if his insulting suggestion, his mouth came down crushingly on hers. She recoiled in revulsion, her skin crawling at his touch as she tried to break his hold on her. At last she managed to twist her head away. 'You disgust me!' Violently she brought her arms up and down again, forcing him to release her and fled away back to the house, intent only on seeking the privacy of her own room.

Her eyes blinded by tears, she didn't see the tall figure standing in the open french windows until she cannoned into him. 'What the hell's going on?' Fraser demanded furiously, dragging her across the hall into his study, too angry to close the door behind him before he was shaking her. 'He *kissed* you!'

Bethan shuddered deeply, her hand coming up to wipe her mouth as if she would wipe away the memory. 'If you think he got me out there to make love to me, you're wrong,' she quavered, on the edge of hysteria. 'Kissing me was only his final insult. Before that he offered me money to take myself off.'

'I'll kill him!' Fraser's livid rage took her by surprise. 'I've taken all I can stand from that man tonight.' He moved towards the door, determination to force a show-down evident in every line of his tense stride, and in that split second, much as she would have liked to see her tormentor measuring his length on the ground, she knew she had to stop it happening.

'No, Fraser, please.' She seized his arm, hanging on when he would have dragged free of her. 'Oh please, it'll only cause more trouble. I should never have told you, and I wouldn't have, only——' She gave a dry sob, knowing it would only fuel his temper if she admitted just how much the incident had upset her. 'Don't you see?' she persisted. 'If you rush out there to my defence, it'll only confirm his suspicions.'

He stopped trying to brush her off and caught her hand. 'What suspicions?'

Too late she could see herself being dragged in deeper. 'Oh, please, can't we just let it drop?' she pleaded.

'What exactly has George Miles been accusing you of?' He put the question softly, almost gently, but there was an implacable note in his voice that told her he meant to have an answer.

'It's all so silly.' Embarrassment put colour into her white cheeks. 'He—he has the ridiculous idea that I'm some sort of *femme fatale* with designs on you, and that you find me more attractive than you should. He—he seems to believe there's something between us. We know it's a ludicrous suggestion, but you must see that if you make an issue over it, Siriol's going to be hurt.' She gazed up at him with drowning green eyes, her vulnerable mouth trembling.

The twist of Fraser's mouth was wry, even while his eyes burned with a strange fire. '*Is* it so ludicrous, Beth? Hasn't there always been something between us? I only ever had to touch you.' His hands slid up her arms to her shoulders, drawing her against him, his head coming down so slowly that surely she could have moved away? And then his mouth was claiming hers, gently, almost tentatively at first, as if relearning the contours, the texture, the taste, and it was too late to deny him as she drowned in a sea of sensual sensation. The passion this one man had always been able to elicit blazed up, burning all the more fiercely for having lain dormant for ten years, within seconds out of control.

The blind response of her mouth and yielding body, of her urgently seeking hands, had him shuddering against her, his kiss deepening with the ravening hunger of a starving man, his arms crushing her possessively, his body enveloping her as if he would absorb it into himself. For Bethan there was no past and no future, just this present terrible aching need to lose herself in this man, to be one with him, part of him forever.

So utterly absorbed were they in needs that had been denied too long, neither heard the door pushed wider. Even Siriol's distressed wail. 'Fraser ... how *could* you?' took several seconds to impinge.

Bethan swayed drunkenly as Fraser let her go, taking longer to come back to earth than he, and it was a crash-landing when she saw the guilt with which he faced his fiancée. 'Siriol ... I'm sorry. I never intended this to happen.'

'What do you mean? You didn't intend to kiss her, or you didn't intend that I should see you doing it?' Siriol challenged tearfully.

'I didn't intend—oh hell!' He swore helplessly, running his hands through his hair. 'Siriol, we have to talk.' He put out a hand appealingly but she struck it away.

'Talk! *Talk!* Were you *talking* to *her*? I hate her. I hate you both!' With a sob she spun on her heel and fled.

'Bethan.' He turned back to her and for one horrified moment she thought he was going to take her in his arms again, to carry on from where his fiancée had interrupted them. Burning with an uncontrollable heat only moments ago, she was now encased in ice, deeply ashamed of her mindless response to Fraser's lovemaking.

Lovemaking! What Fraser had been offering had nothing to do with love. It had been merely lust, and she shouldn't have needed George Miles's warning to tell her that when she had her own experience to go on.

'Beth ... don't go,' he said thickly as she evaded him and reached the door.

But she ignored the plea in his voice as she said bitterly, 'You always did enjoy playing one girl off against another, didn't you, Fraser? Well it looks as if you've done it once too often. If you have any hopes of staying engaged to Siriol, then you'd better go after her.'

'Bethan, I don't want——'

'*You* don't want!' Her anger was all the more bitter for having been allowed that one glimpse of heaven before having it snatched away. 'Fraser, have you any conception of what you've done to that poor girl? How much you've hurt her? Take it from me, I know. I've been there.' She walked quickly away across the hall and up the stairs, leaving him grey-faced.

CHAPTER NINE

A FORTNIGHT later Bethan walked out of the London hospital into the noon-day sun. She felt odd, enormously relieved, and yet still with that niggling unease. She ought to take a taxi to the flat but she was loath to go back there when it made her feel so uncomfortable. Sighing, she knew she had no alternative when there were phone calls she had to make, but to put off the evil moment she decided to walk.

It had been marvellous to see Lorna sitting up and looking so much more like her usual bright self this morning. Last night when they had allowed Bethan a few moments with her she had still been drowsy after the anaesthetic and frighteningly pale and frail from the strain of the operation, and Bethan had felt the weight of responsibility heavy on her shoulders.

Of course Lorna's first question this morning had been to ask if she had heard from Fraser yet, and Bethan had had to admit she hadn't, though she had gone on to assure Lorna she had telephoned her family at Merrifields, and that some of them would be coming to see her today. It hadn't been the answer Lorna wanted to hear, and Bethan knew the older woman was as puzzled and worried by Fraser's inexplicable disappearance as she was herself.

At first, the morning after that dreadful evening when George Miles had come to dinner, Bethan had felt nothing but relief when Lorna told her Fraser had gone off to London. She had no idea whether he had healed the breach wih his fiancée before he left and as she had seen nothing of Siriol or her father either in the ensuing days, she still had no clue. And she told herself it was no business of hers anyway.

167

It was only when, a week after his departure, Dr
Stratton had told Lorna there would be a bed for her at
the hospital the following Thursday, that his absence
became a source of concern. Repeated phone calls to
his London apartment brought no reply, and no one at
Merrifields knew where he was. After several days they
managed to ascertain that he *had* been in London and
had later flown on to Germany, but where he had gone
from there remained a mystery.

In his absence all the arrangements for Lorna's
journey to London and admittance to hospital fell on
Bethan. Not that she minded—the Flowerdews were a
tower of strength, Ernie organising the journey in the
Rover—but apart from the niggling anxiety about
Fraser's well-being, Bethan worried about whether she
was doing things as he would have wanted, especially
when Lorna and Ernie insisted she make herself at
home in Fraser's London flat to be on hand for visiting.

Conveniently situated for the hospital, it wasn't a
large flat, and though tastefully furnished it had no
atmosphere of being a home. When Ernie had taken her
there after they had seen Lorna comfortably settled,
Bethan had felt prickly with embarrassed unease.
Suppose they found Fraser in occupation! But when
Ernie used his key to let them in, the place had an
empty silence.

Ernie showed her round briefly, the sitting-room with
its dining alcove and kitchen leading off, the two
bedrooms with the bathroom in between. He showed her
the larger of the two bedrooms first with its king-size
bed, suggesting this might be the most comfortable for
her, but guessing it was where Fraser slept, she hastily
declined, opting instead for the twin-bedded guest-
room. The thought of using Fraser's bed had a seductive
appeal, but suppose he came back and found her there!

Nevertheless, after Ernie had seen she had everything
she would need and had left to go back to Vine House,
Bethan felt drawn back to the master bedroom.

urnished in shades of brown and cream, it was
ssentially a masculine room, though with little of
raser's impelling personality stamped on it. But for a
nelf of paperback books by the bedhead and a pair of
airbrushes lying on the dressing-table, it could have
een a room in a better-class hotel. Perhaps something
f Fraser himself could be found behind the closed
ardrobe doors, but the urge to look was quelled by the
eeling of being an intruder and she left the room
uickly.

Warming up the pie and fruit tart Molly Flowerdew
ad sent along, Bethan had her dinner and watched
elevision for a while before she went to bed, and still
ne had that uncomfortable feeling of intruding where
ne had no right to be, so much so that she hadn't been
ble to bring herself to unpack. The feeling had still
een with her that morning and she had left the flat
ladly for her visit to the hospital.

Perhaps, she thought, looking up at the façade of the
nodern block when she reached it, she could go out
omewhere for lunch after she had made her phone
alls. The lift whisked her up to the fourth floor and she
ook out the key Ernie had left with her and fitted it
nto the lock. But she hadn't had time to turn it when
ne door was snatched open.

'Where the hell have you been?' Fraser demanded,
lowering at her.

It was a nightmare come true, Fraser coming back to
nd her occupying his flat, but the injustice of his
uestion caught her on the raw. 'Where have I been?
've been visiting your aunt, that's where. Someone had
o organise things while you were gadding about. Lorna
ad her operation yesterday.'

'Yes, I know that.' He closed the door behind her
nd hustled her into the sitting-room. 'I've just come
rom Merrifields. I'm sorry you had all the responsibility
or Lorna, but there were things I had to do. And
nyway, I didn't mean that.' He shook her impatiently.

'I meant where have you been *now*? I rang the hospi[
as soon as I got here and they said you left Lorna ov[
an hour ago.'

Her eyes widened. 'I—I walked.'

'And here I've been imagining you mugged [
knocked down crossing the road.' He ran his han[
through his hair and Bethan was curious to see the sig[
of strain in his face. Had he *really* been worried abo[
her?

'Well, you're here now, so you'd better get packe[
he went on, and her stomach lurched sickeningly. Sh[
had known, of course, that if Fraser came back sh[
would have to move out, but it hurt that he was [
eager to get rid of her.

'I'm sorry if you're annoyed that I've made myself [
home here, but I never actually *un*packed, so it wo[
take a minute to get my things.' She was turning awa[
when he caught her arm.

'Bethan, of course I'm not annoyed. You silly gi[
where else would you have stayed? But right now I'[
taking you to Merrifields.'

'Merrifields!' Bethan stared up at him, her green ey[
mirroring her amazement and dismay. It was the *la[*
place she wanted to go and she couldn't imagine why [
had suggested it. 'Oh, Fraser, I couldn't. Anyway, wh[
about Lorna? I'll find a hotel or boarding-house near[
so I can visit her.'

'Lorna won't lack for visitors,' he said curtly. 'T[
family have worked out a rota system, and of cour[
you'll be able to come back to see her. But until she [
ready to go home, you'll visit her from Merrifields.' H[
hand like a manacle round her wrist he urged her int[
the hallway. 'Which bedroom are you using?'

'The guest-room, of course. But Fraser, really, [
can't . . .'

Her case lay open on one of the chairs, her things st[
folded neatly in it. 'Get your spongebag,' he ordere[
and when Bethan, returning from the bathroom wit[

er toiletries in her hand to find him calmly folding her
nightdress and stowing it away, tried again to protest,
e said quietly but with an odd note of tension, 'Ishbel's
t Merrifields, Bethan. That's where I've been—after I
ettled some urgent business here in London and in
Germany—hurrying her along.' He took her hand in
nis. 'She wants to see you very badly, and Beth, it's
imperative you talk to her.'

She didn't question his last statement, indeed she
nardly heard it. '*Ishbel* . . .' Bethan closed her eyes, the
onging to see her old friend washing over her. But
Merrifields! How could she bear to go there, to all the
memories it held?

As if he understood her hesitation Fraser said
urgently, 'Trust me, Beth. I know I failed you once, but
olease, trust me now.' And something in his voice had
ner bowing her head in silent acquiesence.

Fraser drove fast and mostly without speaking,
oreaking his preoccupation only to ask after her
comfort and to inquire how his aunt had stood up to
he operation. And Bethan was glad of his silence. They
were covering ground she had covered many times in
he past, mostly with Ishbel, sometimes with her
stepfather, occasionally—as now—with Fraser himself,
or, as on the last occasion she had made this journey,
with her stepbrother Mark.

She didn't want to think about Mark and his callous
deception, but on this journey into the past she was
finding many things she would rather have forgotten
crowding her memory. To blot them out she tried to fix
ner mind on Ishbel, but now the meeting with her was
so near she found her palms going moist with
apprehension. They had shared so much in their
growing-up years, been so close. But ten years was a
long time. Ishbel was a wife and mother now, had been
for some time, her life and interests half a world away.
t was inevitable they should have grown apart. Besides,
here was the insuperable barrier of her responsibility

for the death of that child on the night of Ishbel's part
all those years ago between them. However tolerant an
forgiving Ishbel was about it, they could neve
recapture the trusting closeness they had once share
In fact, she wondered why Ishbel had gone to so muc
trouble so they could meet again.

It was only then that Fraser's claim of how badl
Ishbel wanted to see her came back to her, that and h
even more puzzling insistence that it was imperativ
Bethan talked to her. She opened her mouth to ask hi
what he had meant, but at that moment the car turne
into a wide gateway flanked by a lodge and swept alon
the winding drive towards the sprawling old hous
standing on a slight rise.

'I don't think you'll find it much changed,' Frase
said quietly.

'No.' In truth Bethan couldn't see for the tears fillin
her eyes or speak more than that one word for th
thickness in her throat.

The front of the house was bounded by a terrace wit
wide steps leading down to the lawn, the main entranc
being round the back in the courtyard Fraser wa
driving into now, formed by the L-shape of the hous
but he drew the car to a halt in front of a side door i
the shorter arm of the L.

'My cousin Angus and his family have the mai
house now,' he explained. 'Mother and Dad moved int
the wing when Dad retired.'

She had been fond of Fraser's parents but now sh
shrank from seeing them. 'Th-they're here—your parents?

Fraser got out of the car and opened her door
holding her hands firmly as he helped her to her feet
'Stop worrying, Bethan. They've gone to visit Lorna thi
afternoon but they're looking forward very much t
seeing you when they get back. There's only Ishbel her
at the moment.'

'Not—not her family too?'

The pressure of his hands increased. 'Later. They'

be here in a few days but we thought it was important Ishbel should be alone for this meeting.'

If that was meant to be reassuring, Bethan didn't find it so. Only there was no retreat. The door opened and she turned, her heart hammering against her ribs, to see a tall, tanned, superbly groomed young woman standing there, her glossy dark hair expertly cut into a short, sophisticated cap, her clothes proclaiming no expense had been spared. A stranger!

For the space of several heartbeats they stared at each other, and then Ishbel was leaping down the steps with all her old coltish grace, the grin splitting her face so heart-stoppingly familiar that Bethan could almost see the long, dark pigtail she remembered swishing from side to side like the tail of a restless panther.

'Bethan!' Outstretched arms wrapped round her and held her without restraint. 'Oh, Beth, it's *so* good to see you.'

'Ishbel.' Tears filling her eyes and spilling down her cheeks, Bethan clung to her old friend, and it was some time before either of them could bear to draw apart. Slipping Bethan's hand through her arm Ishbel led her into the house, leaving Fraser to bring her suitcase.

'Oh Beth, let me look at you.' Ishbel held her at arm's length while grey eyes so much like Fraser's inspected her lovingly. 'You're so much more fragile than I remember.' Her voice held an aching concern.

Bethan smiled at her, warmed by that concern. 'I'm as tough as an old boot really. It's just that I'm still recovering after a spell in hospital.'

'The injuries you received in Beirut. Yes, Fraser told me.' Ishbel glanced towards the door and Bethan saw that Fraser had followed them into the sitting-room. 'Oh, Beth, we have so much to talk about, and I have something vitally important I must tell you.'

'Hold your horses, Ishbel,' Fraser broke in. 'It's late and I don't think Bethan's had any lunch yet.' He looked at her questioningly.

Bethan shook her head. 'I haven't, but I'm to churned up to eat.'

'Me too,' Ishbel echoed. 'Perhaps when I've got th off my chest. Ever since Fraser told me what ha happened to you that night, my conscience hasn't let n eat or sleep.'

'He told you?' She glanced at him quickly, showir her relief that she didn't have to retell the shaming stor herself. And then she frowned. 'But why should yor conscience trouble you, Ishbel? It was I who got drur and killed that child.'

'But that's the whole point, Beth.' Ishbel's expressio was a mixture of compassion and remorse. 'You didn't

'I think you'd better sit down, Bethan,' Fraser said she stared at his sister blankly.

Hardly aware that he had pushed her gently on to th sofa and had seated himself beside her, his arr protectively round her shoulders, her attention wa wholly on Ishbel who went on, 'And if I hadn't allowe Fraser to rush me off to visit relatives in Australia th morning after my party, no one would have though you had. Even if I'd been told later what they wer accusing you of, I could have come back and told ther the truth.'

'I've already explained why you were kept in th dark, Ishbel,' Fraser broke in tiredly.

'Yes, because you were afraid if I came back t England I'd get mixed up with Mark Latimer again Ishbel paced the rug. 'Maybe you did it from the bes motives, Fraser, but neither of us comes out of this ver well.'

'I really don't understand what you're getting a Ishbel.' Bethan shook her head in bewilderment. 'I ma not remember anything of what happened that nigh but I *do* know the facts. I had way over the limit c alcohol in my blood and I was driving the car tha killed that child.'

'And I'm trying to tell you you *weren't* driving tha

car. You didn't even get drunk of your own volition. That was *my* doing.'

'Oh, now you're being ridiculous,' Bethan burst out disbelievingly. 'It's good to know you're in my corner, Ishbel, but you can't shoulder my guilt.'

'Listen to her, darling. Just shut up and listen.' The endearment and the sudden realisation of Fraser's arm warm round her shoulders brought a prickle to her skin, and she subsided in electric awareness.

'I know I'm not making a good job of explaining, but bear with me, Beth,' Ishbel pleaded. 'Because of my bit of well-meaning interference you've carried that child's death on your conscience for ten years. If I'd had any idea . . .' She swung an easy-chair round to face the couple on the sofa and perched tensely on the edge. 'Beth, you'll remember what a starry-eyed, romantic idiot I was in those days? I was so set on getting you and Fraser together. Well, I knew you loved him and I was pretty sure he felt the same about you. But then he brought that awful Lisa Farraday along to my party. I was furious with him so I worked out this plan. I told him you wanted to see him in the summer-house, and then I told *you* he wanted you to meet *him* there.'

Bethan swallowed a gasped exclamation, but she was unable to do anything about the scorching colour that surged into her cheeks as she thought of the implications of what Ishbel had admitted. Fraser had believed *she* had instigated that meeting! Inwardly she squirmed with mortification as she remembered how wantonly she had thrown herself at him, believing *him* to have arranged the meeting. No wonder he had been so contemptuously scathing when the girl who was more to his taste—the sophisticated Lisa—had come along to bring him to his senses.

So embarrassed was she, she would have moved away from him then, but his arm tightened round her, holding her close, and before he could comment Ishbel was saying miserably, 'Only the whole thing blew up in

my face. It was *Lisa* Fraser came strolling back to the
party with.' She looked accusingly at her brother. 'And
then you disappeared into the library with her for
hours.'

'Only to do some telephoning,' Fraser said tersely.
'Calling the family in Australia to let them know to
expect us and putting things in motion to secure our
flight. I'd seen evidence that night that Mark Latimer
and his friends were into drugs, and I meant to get you
away if I had to do it by force.'

'Yes, well, I didn't know that, did I?' Ishbel conceded
grudgingly. 'And *you* weren't to know that by the end
of that evening I never wanted to see Mark again.
That's why I didn't make any objections about going
with you.

'Anyway.' She picked up the thread again. 'When I
went to look for you, Beth, I found you still in the
summer-house breaking your heart.'

Again embarrassment curled inside Bethan at this
exposure of her youthful feelings, but far from
displaying any embarrassment himself, Fraser's hand
caressed her shoulder in a most disturbing way.

'I couldn't bear you to be so miserable on my
birthday.' Ishbel bit her lip, looking ashamed. 'It was
selfish, I know, but I didn't want anything to spoil my
party. So when Mark suggested spiking the cider-cup
you were drinking with vodka to cheer you up, it didn't
seem such a bad idea. And it worked too. You perked
up no end. But then you got really tight and I began to
worry, though even then I didn't suspect—it was only
when you sparked right out, Beth, that I learned Mark
had been tipping vodka into *all* your drinks.'

Ishbel shuddered. 'I was furious with him, and scared
too. You were unconscious, you see. I wanted to put
you to bed at Merrifields, call Mother or one of the
adults to see if you needed a doctor. But Mark insisted
on taking you home. It wasn't until after I'd helped him
get you into his car I knew why he was so insistent

He—he said if his father saw you in that state it'd cure him of thinking you could do no wrong.' Her mouth twisted in distaste. 'That *really* opened my eyes to what a bastard he was!'

Bethan was aware of Ishbel leaning forward to clasp her hands but her mind was whirling, trying to assimilate what her friend was telling her. 'I know I shouldn't have let him drive off with you without telling anyone,' Ishbel went on earnestly, 'but I was sure your stepfather wouldn't make as much of it as Mark seemed to hope.'

'But—but if I——' Bethan floundered helplessly.

'Exactly.' Fraser's voice was grim. 'If you were unconscious——'

'And you *were*, Beth,' Ishbel broke in. 'Mark had to carry you out to the car and I strapped you into the passenger seat myself.'

'There was no way you could have killed that child, Beth,' Fraser finished, his arm turning her round to face him. 'It was Mark who was driving, Beth. Mark who knocked that little girl off her bike and who then put you into the driving-seat and left you to take the blame, somehow making his own way back to Merrifields. He'd have been careful to keep out of Ishbel's way, of course, but we know from the evidence given at your trial that he begged a lift back to London with one of his friends, complaining bitterly that someone had taken his car.'

It was as if a black pit had opened up at her feet. One part of her mind understood what Fraser and Ishbel were telling her and yet she fought against the knowledge, because to believe it she would have to admit her stepbrother had been guilty of the most appalling callousness.

'You don't *know* that was what happened,' she protested weakly, her eyes wide with horror.

'Oh, yes we do.' Fraser kicked the last tenuous hold on her own guilt away. 'The first thing Ishbel and I did

when we landed at Heathrow this morning was searc[
Mark out. I hadn't seen him for years and I hardl[
recognised him. He's a wreck, Beth, existing from on[
fix to the next. Heroin, I should think. Anyway, [
didn't take much pressure before he was admittin[
everything we've told you is true.'

Bethan gave a harsh, sobbing cry and the black pit a[
her feet yawned wider. For the first time since she ha[
heard of her stepfather's death she could actually fee[
glad he hadn't lived long enough to know the truth; no[
just that his son had let her take the blame for hi[
crime, sentencing her to rejection, loneliness, th[
unbearable weight of guilt. That hardly seemed t[
matter when she couldn't help remembering the polic[
had told her their patrol car had come across th[
accident in the early hours of the morning and by the[
the little girl was dead. What mattered was that if Mar[
had got help at once, the child might have been save[
But he didn't. He had walked away and left that chil[
lying there injured to save his own skin. The enormit[
of it filled her mind, and she slumped as the black pi[
rose up to swallow her.

Consciousness came back slowly, and with it a strang[
feeling of disorientation, as if part of her had bee[
amputated. Her eyelids flickered up and she noted wit[
uncaring detachment she was lying on a bed in [
strange room, while beyond the window the westerin[
sun was a great brazen ball on the horizon. Light[
Golden light dazzling her eyes, seeping into her pores[
flooding her mind and chasing away the last dar[
shadows of guilt, filling her body with its warmth.

She no longer had the death of another human bein[
on her conscience!

She gave a long sigh and immediately there was [
movement at the other side of the bed. Turning he[
head she met Ishbel's anxious gaze. 'Thank goodness[
you've woken at last! We've been so worried.'

Stupidly Bethan's heart leapt at Ishbel's use of the word 'we', but steadied again as she glanced round the room. Obviously Fraser hadn't cared enough to share his sister's vigil. But when had he ever?

'I'm sorry.' She could understand the panic she must have caused. 'I don't know what made me pass out like that.'

'*You're* sorry!' Ishbel fell on her knees beside the bed, clasping Bethan's hand. 'It's *we* who're sorry—Fraser and I. The one person in the world neither of us would have harmed, and between us we ruined your life. Do you think you'll ever be able to forgive us?'

Bethan's eyes widened incredulously. 'What is there to forgive? You couldn't possibly have known how Mark would take advantage of the situation, and as for Fraser, how could *he* be blamed for anything that happened?' Except for not loving her, and she could hardly blame him for that.

'But if I hadn't put vodka into your first drink, if I hadn't let Mark take you home and then gone rushing off to Australia the next day,' Ishbel said remorsefully. 'And I *know* how responsible Fraser feels that in protecting me, he threw you to the wolves.'

Responsible, Bethan thought painfully. That wasn't the kind of feeling she wanted from Fraser. 'What you and Fraser did that night, you both did from the best motives,' she said quietly. 'But if you feel the need of it, then of course I forgive you. As for thinking you ruined my life ... it hasn't all been hard and dangerous, you know. There were some good times and I was able to do some good.'

Wanting to change the subject, she pushed herself up on her elbows. 'I feel an awful fraud, lying here, and I'm absolutely *ravenous*.'

'Well enough to come down to dinner?' Ishbel asked eagerly. 'Mother and Dad are back now and are dying to see you.'

'And I want to see them too.' Bethan smiled in

anticipation, her earlier restraint at the thought of facing them gone. But as she swung her legs off the bed she couldn't resist asking, 'Is Fraser with them? He must have had to carry me up here and I want to thank him.'

'Fraser? No. He's had to run over to Nunsford.' Ishbel sounded casual, but there was a guarded look in her eyes.

It was as if a giant hand were squeezing Bethan's heart. So Fraser had made his peace with Siriol after all, and their engagement was still on. She knew then that subconsciously she had read too much into his concern for her this afternoon, into the endearments he had uttered, the way he had held her. Although the things she had learned today had changed things dramatically for her, altering her view of herself and what she might now hope for herself in the future, she couldn't suppose they had changed anything for Fraser. His sister's traumatic revelations had merely brought out his old protective instincts, that was all.

Squaring her shoulders she stood up. 'Of course, it's Siriol's party tonight, isn't it? Fraser would have to be there.'

'He explained?' Ishbel looked relieved. 'I was afraid you might——'

'Do I have time for a quick shower?' Bethan broke in.

She was proud of the way she got through the evening. From the way she responded to the Lauries' rapturous welcome, talked and laughed over old times, even telling them something of her life over the last ten years, no one would have guessed her heart and mind were thirty miles away where perhaps even now Fraser and Siriol were announcing the date of their wedding.

Ishbel retired to bed early suffering from jet-lag, and her mother urged Bethan to have an early night too. But she was too restless to sleep. With only the bedside lamp casting a soft glow, she sat in her nightdress beside the window, wondering what she was going to do with her future that had so many more possibilities now, except the one she really wanted.

She put Fraser determinedly out of her mind and tried to decide what she was going to do with the rest of her life. She admitted she was a coward, but she knew she could no longer face the life of privation and danger with the relief agency without the scourge of her conscience driving her on. But neither did she think she could settle easily into the routine of nursing in a big hospital. She discounted the idea that one day she might forget Fraser and settle for a lesser love that would allow her to raise her own family, but if she couldn't care for her own children, the next best thing was caring for the children of others. It was then she remembered the letters from a one-time colleague in the relief service telling her about her new job nursing in a mission hospital in Kenya. The small hospital was fairly primitive, Helen had written, and they were chronically understaffed, but it was beautiful country, and peaceful too after some of their assignments, and there was the satisfaction of doing a worthwhile job when some of their patients had to travel a hundred miles or more for treatment.

The headlights of a car coming up the drive attracted her attention, and her heart began to thud heavily as her first thought was that it was Fraser returning. But a glance at her watch showed it was barely midnight. He wouldn't have left Siriol as early as this, even if he intended coming back to Merrifields at all tonight.

But the depth of her longing for him, the power of emotion even thinking about him could conjure up, finally decided her. She would write to Helen offering her services to the mission hospital. Perhaps a job far away from England and all that could remind her of Fraser would eventually help to blunt the pain, help her to forget.

There was a small writing-desk holding paper and

envelopes beside the window. She sat down at it and was halfway down the first page when the door of her room opened.

'I'm sorry if I startled you,' Fraser said as she jumped guiltily, overturning her chair as she shot to her feet. 'But I saw your light was still on.' He strode across the room and picked up the chair she had sent flying. 'What were you doing?' He glanced down at the half-written letter.

What was he doing here? she wondered. He must have left the party early to have driven back by this time, and that surely couldn't have pleased Siriol. She dragged her mind away from futile speculation. 'I—I was writing to a friend in Kenya,' she said in answer to his question. 'She works in a mission hospital there and I'm sounding her out as to the chance of me getting a job there.'

'No!' The single word came with the shocking suddenness of a whip-crack, startling her with its vehemence.

She stared at the deeply etched lines running from his pinched nostrils to the corners of his grim mouth, at what looked uncommonly like censure in his brilliant grey eyes. 'You think I'm being disloyal to the relief agency? But not so long ago you were urging me to give up working for them.'

'Yes—no——' For a few moments he seemed uncharacteristically at loss for words, then, 'I don't see any reason for you to have a job at all,' he said harshly.

'You mean my stepfather's legacy?' From somewhere she dredged up a smile. 'I'm sure I'll find a use for it, but not to live on. I'm ready to admit I'm not up to working where there's war and strife, but Helen assures me this mission is very peaceful. And I have to do *something* with the rest of my life, Fraser.'

'Of course you do,' he agreed quickly. 'But I have an entirely different suggestion to make. Look, perhaps you'd better sit down.' He took her arm and urged her into the chair he had righted, and the heat from his touch seemed to flood her whole body, making her shake with the desire to be in his arms.

'I don't quite know where to start.' He had remained standing, as if he were too keyed up and anxious to relax, and Bethan wondered at it. 'You don't know it, but I think I could have been directly responsible for everything that happened to you ten years ago, Bethan,' he said tightly, amd at once she raised both hands in a defensive gesture as she guessed he was referring to that scene in the summer-house.

'Fraser, I've been through all this with Ishbel,' she protested. 'Neither you nor she can be held responsible for Mark's weakness and malice.'

He caught her hands and held them in a grip that didn't take into account his superior strength. 'Maybe not, but Beth, when Ishbel told me the *true* story of what happened that night—God, I felt so guilty! Because even if I'm wrong and it wasn't my action that sparked the whole thing off, I still bear the responsibility of letting Mark get away with it. One word from me and Ishbel could have blown his lies sky-high. But I said nothing, intent on what I thought were my sister's interests when it was *you* I should have been protecting.'

The word 'responsibility' again, and how it could hurt! More than the physical pain of her crushed fingers. 'It was only natural you should have put Ishbel first. I was nothing more to you than your sister's friend. There was no reason why you should have considered me before her.'

'No reason!' He dropped her hands to rake his own through his hair—a characteristic gesture when he was disturbed—and she surreptitiously rubbed the feeling back into her fingers. 'My God, when I think of all I let you suffer! When I think of those wasted years ... It's more than I can bear!' His eyes were dark with tormented pain.

'I don't consider them wasted,' she objected, thinking only of alleviating his self-reproach.

'Well, I *do*!' he argued fiercely. 'And I want to make it up to you,' he went on, the fierceness dropping away. 'Beth, I told you I had a suggestion to make for your future. I'm asking you to marry me.' He took her hands again, gently this time, and drew her out of the chair. 'I want to spend the rest of my life making sure nothing ever hurts you again.'

For the space of perhaps ten seconds Bethan felt a joy such as she had never experienced before, almost too much to be contained, the joy of every dream she had ever dreamed come true.

Just ten seconds before the cold voice of reason told her it was no such thing. It wasn't *love* that prompted Fraser's proposal but pity, his sense of responsibility. The sound of his shared laughter with Lisa Farraday echoed down the years and she schooled her features, hoping they hadn't already given her away, as she withdrew her hands from his clasp. 'Aren't you forgetting something? You're already engaged to someone else.'

He shook his head, smiling faintly. 'No, my love, not any more.'

She drew in a shocked breath. 'You didn't break your engagement to Siriol tonight—at her party?'

'No, a couple of weeks ago.' He moved impatiently. 'The night she and her father came to dinner. That's why I had to go chasing off to London the next day, to raise new finance for the German project.'

'Yet you still went to her party tonight.' Had that been to try to patch things up, she wondered, and was he only making his offer to herself now because he'd failed?

Dark colour stained his cheekbones. 'You think I wanted to go? She asked me to be there, to save gossip. She didn't want the break made public until after the party.'

Siriol had *asked* him to be there! That put a different complexion on the tangle. 'Don't you think, rather than having face, she might have been having second thoughts?' she suggested carefully. 'Siriol loves you, Fraser.'

His mouth twisted and his eyes burned with frustration. 'Maybe, but I don't return her feelings and she knows it. Siriol's not a girl to accept marriage on those terms.'

In her own dilemma, Bethan had enough compassion to feel sorry for Siriol. What was it about Fraser that he could inspire such love in two women and remain untouched himself? The temptation to settle for what he could offer was overwhelming. She had no doubt he would be a loyal and dutiful husband. But it was his love she wanted, not his pity.

Her chin came up as she put temptation behind her. 'Neither am I. Which is why I can't marry you either, Fraser.'

His face whitened. 'I won't accept that. There's no one else, you admitted as much.'

'No, there's no one else!' She turned away to stare out of the window into the darkened garden, wishing he wasn't making it so hard for her. 'Fraser, today Ishbel relieved me of the burden of guilt I've been carrying for ten years, and now you're asking me to pick up *your* burden. There's only one reason why two people should marry—because they love each other. How do you think I feel, knowing you're only asking me out of a misplaced sense of responsibility?'

'Is *that* what you believe? That I don't love you?' He had moved silently to stand right behind her, his body taut, his voice urgent.

'It's what I *know*,' she said flatly.

He groaned. 'You know nothing! Beth, I've loved you since you were thirteen years old, more green-eyed faun than child. By the time you were eighteen you were an obsession. I wanted you more than I thought it was

possible to want a woman.' His hands fell on h
shoulders and she felt the tremor in his body as he dre
her back against him, his voice thickening. 'I still do.
only have to touch you to go up in flames.'

She closed her eyes, feeling herself weakening at h
insidiously seductive words, the heat of his boo
moulded against her back and the caressing movemen
of his hands on her shoulders bringing a hot surge
desire. Dear God, she wanted to believe him. Yet ho
could she, when the memory of that long-ago rejectic
was still so sharp?

'Why are you saying that when you know it isn
true?' A sob rose in her throat and distress made he
incautious. 'You showed me how little I meant to yc
ten years ago when you looked at me as if I were a litt
trollop and went off to share the joke with you
girlfriend.'

She felt him stiffen, heard his jaggedly indraw
breath, but when she would have moved away from hi
he spun her round, still gripping her shoulders.
thought you said you didn't remember anything abo
the night of Ishbel's party.' Shocked eyes burned in
white face.

'Nothing that came after, no, but being with you
the summer-house? Oh, yes. It was the only thing
could remember when I woke up to find myself
hospital.' She lowered her head, staring fixedly at th
pleated front of his dress shirt. 'So don't try to preten
you wanted me, Fraser. I was yours for the taking the
but you turned me down in favour of Lisa Farraday
more experienced charms. You even *laughed* at me wit
her!'

'No!' His strangled denial had her head jerking u
again but the bitter words on her lips died when she sa
the shattered expression on his face, the greyness of h
skin. 'Beth, it wasn't like that. No listen, please listen
he begged as she would have repudiated his assertion.
wanted you. God, how I wanted you! But I'd promise

our stepfather I'd wait. He was afraid of me tying you
down too young. That's why I kept girls like Lisa
around, as camouflage, so my obsession for you didn't
get out of hand. But then that night you were so lovely,
responded to me so sweetly. If I hadn't called a halt
when I did, you'd have *had* to marry me, even if you
weren't ready for it.'

Bethan swayed dizzily. '*Marry* you?' she said faintly.

Fraser's arms tightened round her. 'Oh, my darling,
'd known for a year or more you were the wife I wanted.
But apart from Charles asking me not to rush you,
there was the problem of Ishbel's involvement with
your stepbrother. How could I go on insisting he was a
bad influence on her if I was guilty of seducing you?
Anyway, it seemed then that there was plenty of time to
settle things between us, once I'd got Ishbel sorted out.
Only there *was* no time.' Suddenly his voice was bleak.
I played into Mark's hands and I lost you.'

It was as if someone had shaken a kaleidoscope,
shifting the picture she had carried with her so long,
altering it out of all recognition. Fraser had wanted to
marry her! He had cared about her after all! A glow
started in her heart, a spreading warmth of happiness
such as she had never known before. And she was
afraid of it! She wanted to give in to it and let it take
her but she didn't dare, and she trembled as she
reminded him chokingly, 'You laughed at me. You
can't deny it, Fraser, I heard you, laughing with Lisa.'

'Not at you, Beth. Never at you, you must believe
me. The last thing I wanted was for Lisa to know you
were in the summer-house. I can't remember what I
said to her, but it was something about my sister
sending me on a wild-goose chase. All these years and
you've thought——' He groaned, his hands coming up
to cup her face, his thumbs moving with caressing
tenderness against her cheeks. 'Oh, my sweet love ... I
did you so much damage. How can I ever expect you to
forgive me?'

There was such a wealth of grief in his voice sh
could no longer doubt his sincerity and quickly she p
her fingers over his lips. 'Don't. Oh, don't talk lik
that.'

'You *will* forgive me?' He caught her wrists an
kissed her palms with such ardent reverence it shoo
Bethan to the core. 'Beth, I used to flatter myself onc
that you were beginning to love me. Is there any hop
for me now? Because I don't think I would want to g
on living if I lost you again.'

She hadn't known happiness could be so painfu
tearing the heart out of her. She lifted her face, her eye
shining like wet emeralds through her tears as sh
slipped her arms round his neck. 'I loved you ther
Fraser, and within hours of meeting you again, I knew
loved you still,' she said simply. 'I suppose I alway
will.'

With a hoarse groan of thankfulness he gathered he
to him, his mouth taking possession of hers in a kis
that blotted out the years of anguish. There was onl
the conflagration that was consuming them, the flame
licking higher and higher, and when the room tilte
round her as he swept her off her feet and carried her t
the bed it seemed only right that the passion that ha
sprung up between them so long ago at Merrifiel
should be consummated here too; a passion that ra
too swiftly out of control and made the first time fo
Bethan a mixture of pleasure and pain. But even tha
couldn't dim the new, unaccustomed joy. And later
when he loved her again, he took her to suc
unimagined heights she couldn't seem to stop tremblin
as she lay in his arms afterwards.

'What is it, my darling?' Fraser's forehead pleated i
concern, his eyes searching her face. 'Did I hurt you?'

She shook her head quickly to dispel his anxiety. 'It'
just that—I don't think I know *how* to be happy.' He
hands moved against his hair-roughened chest, the taut
muscled shoulders, as if she couldn't believe the evidenc

of her senses. 'I keep thinking this *has* to be a dream, that in a minute I'll wake up and it'll all be gone, and I'm afraid.'

Her voice broke as he hugged her possessively. 'Oh my little love.' His voice was ragged with emotion. 'Do you think I don't feel like that too? That's why I couldn't wait.' One arm loosened its grip and his hand came round to tip her chin until she was looking directly into his clear grey eyes. 'Tomorrow, my darling, we do something about getting a special licence, but I make you this vow now. I love you with all my heart and body, my mind and soul, and never, *ever*, will I allow you to be lonely and afraid again. I shall love you till the end of time, and you *will* be happy.'

Slowly the trembling stilled as the tension seeped out of her to be replaced by a growing confidence, and what began as a glimmering smile as she felt the strength of his arms about her, the power of his body against her softness, widened into glowing trust. 'I believe you,' she breathed.

Here's how to get this special offer from Harlequin!

January
BETTY NEELS
TREASURY EDITION
COUPON

As simple as 1...2...3!

1. Each month, save one Treasury Edition coupon from your favorite Romance or Presents novel.
2. In four months you'll have saved four Treasury Edition coupons (only one coupon per month allowed).
3. Then all you have to do is fill out and return the order form provided, along with the four Treasury Edition coupons required and $2.95 for postage and handling.

Mail to: Harlequin Reader Service

In the U.S.A.
901 Fuhrmann Blvd.
P.O. Box 1397
Buffalo, NY 14240

In Canada
P.O. Box 609
Fort Erie, Ontario
L2A 9Z9

BN-Jan-2

Please send me my Special copy of the Betty Neels Treasury Edition. I have enclosed the four Treasury Edition coupons required and $2.95 for postage and handling along with this order form. (Please Print)

NAME_____

ADDRESS_____

CITY_____

STATE/PROV._____ZIP/POSTAL CODE_____

SIGNATURE_____
This offer is limited to one order per household.

SUPPLIES LIMITED

This special Betty Neels offer expires
February 28, 1987.

ATTRACTIVE, SPACE SAVING BOOK RACK

Display your most prized novels on this handsome and sturdy book rack. The hand-rubbed walnut finish will blend into your library decor with quiet elegance, providing a practical organizer for your favorite hard-or soft-covered books.

Only $9.95

Approximately 16" x 8 when assembled

Assembles in seconds

To order, rush your name, address and zip code, along with a check or money order for $10.70* ($9.95 plus 75¢ postage and handling) payable to *Harlequin Reader Service*:

Harlequin Reader Service
Book Rack Offer
901 Fuhrmann Blvd.
P.O. Box 1325
Buffalo, NY 14269-1325

Offer not available in Canada.

*New York residents add appropriate sales tax.

BYB-1B